Grover Shipton
1928

Grover
Shipton

JERRY TODD AND THE TALKING FROG

MR. RICKS ABSENT-MINDEDLY POURED THE SYRUP DOWN THE BACK OF HIS NECK AND SCRATCHED HIS PANCAKE!

Jerry Todd and the Talking Frog. *Frontispiece—*(*Page* 12)

JERRY TODD
AND THE
TALKING FROG

BY

LEO EDWARDS

AUTHOR OF
THE JERRY TODD BOOKS, ETC.

ILLUSTRATED BY

BERT SALG

GROSSET & DUNLAP
PUBLISHERS : : NEW YORK

Made in the United States of America

JERRY TODD SAYS:

When I started writing this book, I thought of calling it: JERRY TODD AND THE PUZZLE ROOM MYSTERY. But Scoop told me that wasn't the proper title. "There is more in the book about the talking frog than there is about the puzzle room," he pointed out. "So why don't you call it JERRY TODD AND THE TALKING FROG?"

So it was our leader, you see, who gave this book its title.

Like my other books, this is a fun-mystery-adventure story. The "fun" part is where we peddle the spy's beauty soap. Bubbles of Beauty, let me tell you, was very wonderful soap! At first we couldn't believe that it would do all of the amazing things that Mr. Posselwait claimed for it. But that is where *we* got a surprise!

There is a ghost in this story. B-r-r-r-r! At midnight it comes to the old haunted house, walking on the porches. Creepy, I'll tell the world. We kept the doors locked. For we were all alone in the brick house, Scoop and I and Peg and our new chum, Tom Ricks. It was to help our new chum that we braved the perils of the haunted house. You see, a puzzle maker had met with a strange death in the brick house, and that is what made it haunted.

"Ten and ten." That was the Bible's secret. What was "ten and ten"? Why did the ghost come nightly to the inventor's home? We found out, but it took us many exciting days to solve the mystery.

Yes, if you like a spooky, shivery, mysterious story, you surely will enjoy this book, my fifth one.

Here are the titles of my five books in their order:

JERRY TODD AND THE WHISPERING MUMMY

JERRY TODD AND THE ROSE-COLORED CAT

JERRY TODD AND THE OAK ISLAND TREASURE

JERRY TODD AND THE WALTZING HEN

JERRY TODD AND THE TALKING FROG

My sixth book will be JERRY TODD AND THE PURRING EGG. This dodo egg, taken from King Tut's tomb, was more than three thousand years old. The Tutter newspaper called it the "million-dollar egg." Could it be rejuvenated? One man said so. The story of what happened when the egg was "rejuvenated" makes mighty good reading for a boy who likes a book packed full of chuckles and mysterious tangles.

Your friend,

JERRY TODD.

CONTENTS

JERRY TODD AND THE TALKING FROG

CHAPTER I

THE BOY IN THE TREE

I GOT into the bushes quick as scat. Biting hard on my breath, sort of. For right there in front of our eyes was a regular old gee-whacker of a dinosaur. Bigger than the town water tower and the Methodist Church steeple put together. I tell you it was risky for us.

My chum got ready with his trusty bow and arrow.

"Do you think you can hit him in the heart?" I said, excited-like, squinting ahead to where the dinosaur was dragging his slimy body out of the pond.

Scoop Ellery's face was rigid.

"Got to," he said, steady-like. "If I miss, he'll turn on us and kill us both."

"It's a lucky thing for Red and Peg," I said, thinking of my other chums, "that they aren't in it."

"They'll miss us," said Scoop, "if we get killed."

My thoughts took a crazy jump.

"Why not aim for a tickly spot in his ribs," I snickered, pointing to the dinosaur, "and let him giggle himself to death?"

"Sh-h-h-h!" cautioned Scoop, putting out a hand. "He's listening. The wind is blowing that way. He smells us."

"What of it?" I grinned. "We don't smell bad."

"Keep still," scowled Scoop, "while I aim."

Bing! went the bow cord. My eyes followed the arrow. It struck. The old dinosaur angrily tooted his horn. But he didn't drop dead. For his hide was sixteen inches thick.

We were lost! Scoop said so. And without arguing the matter I went lickety-cut for a tree.

"Come on!" I yipped over my shoulder. "He's after us."

Up the tree I went monkey-fashion. And when I straddled a limb and squinted down, there was the old dinosaur chewing my footprints off the tree trunk.

"How much longer have we got to live?" I panted.

"Two minutes and fifteen seconds," informed Scoop, who, of course, had followed me into the tree.

"I can't die that quick," I told him. "For I'm all out of wind."

But he was squinting down at the dinosaur and seemed not to hear me.

"He's got his trunk coiled around the tree," he said. "Feel it shake! He's pulling it up by the roots."

"Wait a minute; wait a minute," I said, motioning the other down. "You're getting things muddled. A dinosaur hasn't got a trunk. This must be a hairy elephant."

"Climb higher," cried Scoop. "He's reaching for us."

So up we went.

All of a sudden I heard some one go, "Hem-m-m!" And what do you know if there wasn't another boy in the top of the tree! A stranger. About our age.

"You had me guessing," he said, grinning

good-natured-like. "I thought at first you were crazy."

Staring, I finally managed to get my tongue unhooked.

"Where'd you come from?" I bit off, letting my face go dark. For he didn't belong in our dinosaur game. And I wanted him to know it.

Instead of answering, he inquired pleasantly:

"Was that a cow that chased you up the tree?"

"Huh!" I grunted, letting myself go stiff. "Do you suppose we'd run from a cow?"

"It made a noise like a cow," he grinned, "when you shot it with your toy bow and arrow."

"It's a dinosaur," I scowled.

His grin spread wider.

"And it was a dodo bird," he said, "that picked me up by the seat of the pants and dropped me in the top of this tree."

Well, that kind of took my breath. And I glared at him for a moment or two. Then his steady, friendly grin put me to laughing.

"I saw you coming through the woods," he said after a moment. "I couldn't quite figure out what you were doing. So I climbed up here to watch."

Something poked a green snout from the stranger's right-hand coat pocket.

"Are you after frogs, too?" he inquired, following my eyes.

"Frogs?" I repeated, staring harder at the squirming pocket.

He pointed down to the pond in the ravine.

"It's full of frogs," he told me. "Big fellows. See?" and producing an old lunker of a bullfrog he held it up.

"Hello!" he said.

"K-k-kroak!" responded the frog.

The boy laughed.

"Perfect," he said, patting the frog on the head. "Now say it in Chinese. *Hello!*"

"K-k-kroak!"

The grinning eyes looked into mine.

"Would you like to hear him say it in Yiddish?"

"I'd like to make a meal of his fried legs," I returned.

"You can have him," the other offered. Then, without another word, he let himself down limb by limb, scooting in the direction of town, a mile away.

Scoop gave a queer throat sound and came out of his thoughts.

"That's the new kid," he said.

"You talk like you know him."

"I know of him. He belongs to the new family

in the old Matson house. Ricks is the name on the mailbox. There's a man and a woman and this boy in the family—only the woman is a Miss Polly Ricks, and not the boy's mother. The mother is dead, I guess."

Then my chum told me how his pa was the administrator of the Matson estate; and, of course, it was through Mr. Ellery, a Tutter storekeeper, that the new family had rented the long-vacant house where Mr. Matson, a queer old man, had been murdered for his money. It is a lonely brick house on the edge of town. The front yard is full of pine trees, just like a cemetery. And when the wind blows the pines whisper strange stories about the murder and about the vanished body.

It is no place for people to live. Everybody in Tutter says so. And I wondered why this new Ricks family had picked out such a lonely, spooky home.

It was a queer move for them to make.

We talked it over and exchanged opinions on the way into town. And when we came to the grove of pine trees, Scoop took me through a hole in the hedge and pointed out a brand new lock on the barn door.

A queer, droning sound weighted the air. I called the other's attention to it.

"Machinery," said Scoop, nodding toward the east wing of the big barn. "Not farm machinery," he explained, "but lathes for turning steel, and drillers. Pa helped unload the truck."

"Mr. Ricks must be a machinist," I said.

"I have a hunch," said Scoop, "that he's an inventor."

CHAPTER II

THE TALKING FROG

THE following Monday morning the new boy started to school, entering our grade. And in the days that immediately followed I came to like Tom Ricks a lot. For he was the right sort. And soon we were visiting back and forth, playing in my yard one night and in his the next.

Scoop, of course, shared in our games, as did Red Meyers and Peg Shaw, my other chums. For I never would throw down an old friend for a new one. And it was during one of our trips to the old Matson place that we learned about the talking frog.

For Mr. Ricks, an inventor as Scoop had surmised, was working on a very wonderful radio toy. Tom called it an electro-mechanical frog.

We had promised our new chum that we wouldn't breathe a word about the talking frog to any one else. For a Chicago radio company had spies searching for Mr. Ricks. These people knew that the inventor was working on a radio toy, and it was their evil intention to steal the invention, the same as they had stolen a simplified radio transmitter that Mr. Ricks had designed and built in his little Chicago workshop. It was to save the new invention from being stolen from him that he was now hiding in our inland town, where he could work undisturbed.

"A Milwaukee company is interested in Pa's invention," Tom told us, "and if he can make the frog say, 'Hello!', or make it repeat any other single word, they'll pay him twenty-five thousand dollars for the idea and develop it in their laboratories."

Grinning, he added:

"So you can see what I had in my mind that day in the tree. I frequently get frogs for Pa, to guide him in tuning the tone bars. For the toy, of course, must sound like a real frog or it won't be a complete success."

"And you say the mechanical frog actually talks?" said Scoop, who had been eagerly taking in each word.

"Sometimes it does," said Tom. "But you can't depend on it. You see it isn't perfected." There was a short pause. "I tell you what: Come out to-night after supper and I'll try and coax Pa to let you see it. I'll explain to him that he can trust you to keep his secret."

"Hot dog!" cried Peg Shaw, thinking of the fun we were going to have listening to the talking frog.

This was on Friday. And directly after supper Scoop and I and Peg headed for Tom's house. Red couldn't go. He had queer spots all over his back. Not knowing whether it was scarlet fever or mosquito bites, his mother was keeping him in the house until the doctor had seen him.

"You fellows are lucky," he told us, when we called for him.

"*You* will be lucky," his mother told him sharply, "if you escape an attack of scarlet fever. For there's dozens of cases over in Ashton. And you were there last week."

"Aw! . . . I haven't got a fever. Please let me go, Ma."

"You'll go to bed," his mother threatened, "if you don't keep still."

We had met Aunt Polly in the times that we had been at Tom's house, but never had we seen Mr. Ricks until to-night. He was considerably taller than his sister, and older, with stooped shoulders and faded blue eyes that looked meekly at one over the top of small, steel-rimmed spectacles.

Tom introduced us. But he had to speak to his father several times and shake him by the shoulder to make the old gentleman put aside his book. It was a book on inventions, I noticed.

"Oh, yes; yes, indeed," said Mr. Ricks, vague-like, giving us a limp handclasp without actually seeing us. "Very glad to meet you. Very glad, of course. Um. . . . Now whar did I leave off?" and plunk! went his nose into the big book.

Later we came to know how very absent-minded he was, and how queer in a lot of his actions; but I am going to tell you about it here, before I go deeper into my story, else you might not fully understand what follows.

For instance, he never seemed able to quit thinking about his inventions. Even while eating his meals an idea would come to him, and there he would sit with his fork halfway to his mouth, his eyes making invisible drawings of things in the air. And you would be talking with him about the weather, or about fishing, and right in the middle of a sentence he would mumble: "Now if I file the end sharp, I bet it'll work easier an' won't bind," or, "Um. . . . I bet I've got one tooth too many in that thar gear."

I guess he wouldn't have known enough to stop working at mealtime and bedtime if Aunt Polly, in her bustling capable way, hadn't kept tab on him. And he needed some one like that to give him sharp attention. For I've seen him absent-mindedly hang his handkerchief on the towel rack and stuff the towel in his pocket. And once, going to church, he got as far as the front gate before his watchful sister discovered that he had on one shoe and one slipper. Golly Ned! It would have been fun to see him come into church dressed like that.

Peg tells the story, which he made up, I guess, that one time when he was eating breakfast at Tom's house, Mr. Ricks absent-mindedly poured the syrup down the back of his neck and scratched his pancake!

To-night Aunt Polly bustled from window to window, drawing the shades.

"Now," she nodded sharply to the inventor, who was pottering at her heels, book in hand, "you can bring it in."

The lowering of the window shades had filled me with uneasiness. For the precaution suggested the near-by presence of possible prying eyes. And I didn't like to think of the shadowy pines as holding such hidden dangers.

Then my nervousness melted away in the moment that the talking frog was placed on a small table in the middle of the room. Made of metal and properly shaped and painted, it squatted five inches high, which was considerably larger than a live frog, but it had to be oversize, Tom explained, because of the many gears, magnets and tone bars that his father had designed to go inside.

We had our noses close. And no movement of the inventor's escaped us as he wound a spring here and turned a knob there. It was a pretty fine invention I thought. And I realized that Mr. Ricks, with all of his queer forgetful ways, was a very smart man. He was what you would call a genius. I guess that is the right word.

Presently the worker straightened, sort of satisfied-like, so we knew that the frog was ready to perform.

"Hello!" he said, talking into the green face, his chin thrust out.

The vibration of his voice tripped the machinery and put the wheels into motion. The big hinged mouth opened in a natural way. But other than a dull rumbling of gears, no sound came out.

"Jest you wait," puttered Mr. Ricks. "I hain't got it 'justed quite right."

We watched him.

"Hello!" he said, after a moment.

"R-r-r-r!" responded the frog.

Aunt Polly laughed good-naturedly.

"Laws-a-me! It sounds as though it had a bad pain in its tin stomach."

"Indigestion," grinned Peg, his big mouth stretching from ear to ear.

"We should have brought along some charcoal tablets," laughed Scoop.

The disappointed inventor did some more puttering. But all that he could get out of the tin frog was, "R-r-r-r!"

"It did better than that last night," Tom told his father.

"I know it, Tommy. I know it. Um. . . . Calc'late the new tone bar that I made to-day hain't improved it none."

He puttered with the frog for maybe an hour. Finally Aunt Polly took up her knitting and told him to put the frog in the kitchen cupboard. She had noticed, I guess, that he was getting nervous.

"Mebby," he countered, fidgety-like, "I better put it in the barn."

I grinned. For I saw in a moment what he

was up to. He wanted to keep on tinkering, and he would have that chance if he could get the frog into his workshop.

But Aunt Polly read the other's thoughts.

"I said to put it in the kitchen cupboard," she repeated firmly.

The blue eyes offered meek protest.

"It'll be safer in the barn, Polly."

"It'll be safe enough in the kitchen," said Aunt Polly, jabbing with her needles.

"Yes, of course; of course. But I've got a burglar 'larm on the barn door. Mebby, Polly——"

"And I've got a burglar alarm on the kitchen door," cut in Aunt Polly, making her needles fly.

A domino game failed to draw our thoughts from the talking frog; and Tom told us how the Milwaukee company was planning to get out a complete line of talking toys—this in the event that Mr. Ricks' experiments were successful.

"It seems to me," said Scoop, out of his thoughts, "that twenty-five thousand dollars isn't enough money for such a big idea."

"Twenty-five thousand dollars," spoke up Peg, whose folks are poor, "is a fortune, I want to tell you!"

"Of course," nodded Scoop. "But an invention

like this ought to be worth more than twenty-five thousand dollars to the man who thought it up. A hundred thousand, I should say. Or half a million."

"I forgot to tell you," Tom said, "about Pa's royalty."

"Royalty?" I repeated.

"It's this way," Tom explained. "Pa'll get twenty-five thousand dollars cash money for the idea; then the company will develop and apply the idea, and Pa'll get a royalty on each talking toy sold."

I asked what a royalty was.

"It's a written agreement," Tom told me, "under which Pa'll get a certain part of every dollar that the company takes in. The money is his pay, as an inventor, for letting them use his idea. For instance, if they sell a million dollars' worth of talking toys, Pa'll get fifty thousand dollars. That's five per cent."

"Crickets!" I said, regarding my new chum with quickened interest. "You're going to be rich."

He sobered.

"I hope so, Jerry. I'd like to know what it seems like to be rich. We've been poor all my life. And I've got a hunch that Aunt Polly won't be able to stretch our money over very many more months. Yes, if Pa doesn't hurry up and make his frog talk, I suspect that we're likely to move over to the county poorhouse."

It was now after nine o'clock and time for Scoop and Peg and me to go home. So we got our caps. But in the moment that we started for the front door a fearful racket came from the kitchen. Bing! *Crash!* BANG! It sounded as though a million tin pans had been upset in a heap. I pretty nearly jumped out of my skin.

"My burglar alarm!" screeched Aunt Polly, throwing her knitting into the air. And like a flash she disappeared fearlessly into the hall, heading for the back room.

CHAPTER III

AN UNKNOWN PROWLER

SQUEEZING the stutter out of my nerves, I followed Tom and my chums into the kitchen. The back door was ajar. Some one had picked the lock. But in opening the door the unknown prowler had not reckoned on Aunt Polly's home-made burglar alarm—a dozen or more pots and pans balanced nicely on a wabbly stepladder.

"Um. . ." mumbled Mr. Ricks, pottering into the room, book in hand. "Did I hear a noise?" Looking over his glasses, he got his eyes on the pans and stared at them blankly. "Now how did all them pans come to fall down? An' whar in Sam Hill did they fall from?" Mouth open, he stared at the ceiling, moving in a small circle.

Aunt Polly caught him as he stumbled over a pan.

"Shut the door," she told Tom crisply, "and lock it." Then she took the pottering inventor by the arm and led him from the room. "Go back to your book," she ordered. "We don't need you here."

"But, Polly——"

She got him out of the kitchen. Then she sort of went to pieces.

"Oh, Tommy!" she cried, trembling, her eyes filled with fear. "It's one of Gennor's spies. You know how they've been searching the country for your pa. They've come to steal his invention. What shall we do?"

"I wish I knew," said Tom, looking dizzy.

Scoop's eyes were snapping.

"Why," he spoke up, taking the lead, sort of, "the thing for us to do is to save the frog."

Aunt Polly gave a gesture of despair.

"We might as well give up," she cried, sinking into a chair. "For we stand no chance against Gennor."

Scoop wanted to know who Gennor was.

"Mr. Felix Gennor," Tom informed, "is the president of the Gennor Radio Corporation of Chicago."

"The name sounds big," said Scoop. "He must have a lot of money."

"Millions," informed Tom, gloomy-like.

"Which means," said Scoop, sizing up the situation in his quick way, "that it's going to be a hard fight to lick him."

Aunt Polly was wringing her hands.

"We stand no chance," she repeated, shaking her head. "For money always wins out."

"Money won't win out this trip," declared Scoop.

After a bit the conversation slowed up and we told Aunt Polly that she had best go to bed and get some rest.

Scoop did the talking.

"You mustn't worry," he told her, as she started up the stairs with a hand lamp, "for there's no immediate danger. And by to-morrow morning we'll know what to do to save Mr. Ricks' invention."

It was his scheme for the four of us to stand guard till daybreak. So, when Aunt Polly and Mr. Ricks were in bed, I 'phoned to Mother, explaining that I would spend the night with Tom. Then Scoop and Peg 'phoned in turn to their folks.

Making sure that the doors and windows were locked, we took the talking frog from the cupboard and buried it in a wooden box in the cellar's dirt floor. We intended, as guards, to see that no one entered the house without our knowledge;

but, as Scoop sensibly pointed out, it was just as well to play safe and keep the invention under cover.

In the next hour our leader sifted his thoughts for a plan to outwit the Chicago manufacturer. And finally he waggled, as though having come to certain satisfactory conclusions.

"One time," he said, "my Uncle Jasper invented a percolating coffee pot and got it patented in Washington. The patent prevented any one else from stealing his invention. . . . Is your pa's talking frog patented?" he inquired, looking into Tom's face.

"Of course not. It isn't perfected yet."

"Everything seems to work all right except the tone bars."

"Yes."

"Well, let's get a patent on the parts that work. For that is what Gennor would immediately do if he got his hands on the frog. If we get to Washington first with our patent application he'll be licked."

Tom's eyes snapped.

"You're right. I'll tell Pa about it the first thing in the morning."

"Yes," waggled Scoop, "your pa is the one to see about the patent. And the sooner he starts for Washington the better. There's a train into Chicago at five o'clock. And from Chicago he can go directly to Washington. The people in the patent office will tell him how to get his drawings registered. And while he's doing that, we'll have some fun with mister millionaire."

"A thing I can't understand," mused Tom, "is how Gennor traced Pa to this town."

"Maybe," I spoke up, giving Scoop and Peg the wink, "it was a ghost that picked the lock, and not a spy as you suppose."

"Ghost?" repeated Tom, staring.

"Mr. Matson's ghost," I followed up.

"Who's Mr. Matson?" he wanted to know.

"Haven't you heard about the murder?" I countered, surprised.

He shook his head.

"Mr. Matson," I told him, "was a queer old codger. A puzzle maker. Didn't believe in banks. Kept his money in the house. One night robbers came. The old man was murdered. But the body never was found. That's the strange part. The robbers either buried it or took it away with them."

"Then how do you know there was a murder?"

"Because the cellar stairs and the kitchen floor were covered with blood. Big puddles of it.

And the money and the ten-ring puzzle were gone."

Tom scratched his head.

"But I don't get you," he said, puzzled. "Even if there was a murder, why should the old man's ghost come *here?*"

"Because," I said, putting my voice hollow, "right here in this kitchen is where they cut his throat. This was his home."

Tom's eyes bulged. And noticing this, Scoop laughingly clapped a hand on the frightened one's shoulders.

"Jerry's trying to scare you, Tom. No one ever saw the old man's ghost around here."

"Old Paddy Gorbett did," I reminded quickly.

"Shucks! Any one who knows old Paddy always believes the opposite to what he tells."

Tom shrugged and gave a short laugh.

"I've read stories about ghost houses, but I never thought I'd live in one."

"There's no such thing as a ghost," declared Scoop.

"Of course not," agreed Tom. "But just the same we had better keep this story from Aunt Polly's ears. It would make her nervous. And she has plenty of worries as it is. If Pa goes to Washington, she won't sleep a wink till he gets back. She'll imagine him getting into all kinds of trouble."

We thought naturally that the mysterious prowler would make further attempts to enter the house. But daybreak came without a single disturbing sound.

At four o'clock Tom awakened his aunt. She readily admitted to the wisdom of getting the talking frog drawings registered in the patent office at Washington; but the thought of sending her absent-minded brother so far from home worried her.

"I just know that something awful will happen to him," she declared.

But Tom won her over. And then between them they made the dazed inventor understand what was expected of him.

It was daylight when we went with Mr. Ricks to the depot. I was on needles and pins, sort of, expecting any second to have a spy jump out and grab the old gentleman before we could get him on the cars. Therefore I drew a breath of relief when the train pulled out.

But a shock awaited us when we ran up the path to the house.

"He didn't get the right papers at all," Aunt Polly cried from the front porch. "His drawings are in there on the table. And what he has is a roll of my dress patterns."

Well, we were struck dumb, sort of. For, with Mr. Ricks aboard the speeding train, what chance had we to exchange the useless dress patterns for the needed drawings? None. Our helplessness made me sick.

"He'll discover the mistake when he gets to Washington," Scoop said finally, "and wire us. Then we can mail the drawings, registered. It will delay matters; but it's the best thing that we can do under the circumstances."

"Tom's pa never sent a telegram in all his life," waggled Aunt Polly. "He won't know how."

Nevertheless a telegram came that afternoon. Scoop read it aloud. There was a dead silence. Then Tom went in search of his relative.

"Aunt Polly," he said, "you've got to get ready for a trip."

"Laws-a-me!" gasped the old lady, suspecting the truth. "What awful thing has happened to your pa?"

"He took the wrong train out of Chicago. And how he ever happened to get off at Springfield, Illinois, I don't know. But he's there—the telegram says so. And the dress patterns have come up missing."

"Gennor's work!" cried Aunt Polly, acting as though she was ready to collapse.

Tom nodded grimly.

"Pa is no match for the crooks. And you've got to go to him and help him. They won't get the real drawings away from *you*. And you can stay in Washington till the drawings have been registered in the patent office."

"But why don't you go?" Aunt Polly wanted to know, with a troubled look.

Tom regarded her steadily.

"I have a hunch," he said, "that I'm going to be needed here."

"But I don't like to go away and leave you alone."

Scoop came into the conversation with an easy laugh.

"Don't let that worry you, Aunt Polly. For he won't be alone. We're going to stand by him. Hey, gang?"

"Easy," said Peg.

"How about you, Jerry?"

"Easy," I said, copying after Peg.

I tried to act chesty about it. But I didn't succeed very well. For I was thinking about the man with the million dollars.

CHAPTER IV

WE TAKE THE FROG TO SCHOOL

Aunt Polly put her railroad ticket into her handbag.

"Now," she told Tom, fumbling nervously with the handbag's metal clasp, "try and keep yourself nice and neat while I'm away and wash behind your ears and don't be late to school and feed the canary and the goldfish and wind the clock Sunday night."

"I'll remember," Tom grinned.

"There's plenty of baked stuff in the pantry and half of a ham and you know how to fry potatoes and boil eggs. So I warrant you won't starve. But in lighting fires be careful with your matches and don't burn down the house."

Tom waggled, still grinning.

"And feed the cat," his aunt continued, "and don't let the sun shine through the windows on the parlor carpet and——"

Here the train for Springfield rumbled into the station.

"Good-by, Aunt Polly," said Tom, as the excited little old lady went briskly up the car steps.

Pausing, she bent over and gave him a kiss on the mouth. Then her forehead puckered.

"There was something else I wanted to tell you," she said, thoughtful-like, "but it's plumb slipped my mind."

"All aboard!" called the conductor.

"Oh, yes," screeched Aunt Polly, as the train got into motion, "it's my rubber plant. Water it every day and put dish water on it once a week and——"

In the silence that followed the train's departure, Tom grinned at us and drew a deep breath.

"She forgot to tell me to keep the ice box door closed and not to let the cat sleep on the parlor sofa."

Then he sobered.

"But Aunt Polly's all right. And I don't want you to think that I'm making fun of her. Ginks! I'll miss her like sixty. And I'll be glad when this patent office business is over with so that she and Pa can be home again."

As we turned to leave the station the Stricker gang scooted by us. We haven't any time for the Strickers. Bid and Jimmy are cousins and one is just as mean and as tricky as the other. That part of Tutter beyond Dad's brickyard is called Zulu-town, and it is in this tough neighborhood that the Strickers and their followers have their homes. Because we won't do the mean things they do they have it in for us.

"Aunty has gone away on the choo-choo," hooted Bid, "and left her 'ittle boy home all alone."

"And she gave him a nice juicy kiss," jeered Jimmy.

"Right on the mouth," another member of the gang put in.

Tom took after them, chasing them away.

It was darkening fast, so we started back to the brick house. First, though, I ran home and explained the situation to Mother. She immediately wanted to know why Tom couldn't come to our house and stay. I told her that it would be more fun living at his place—sort of like camping. She shook her head and said that boys were queer creatures.

"Did you know," she told me, "that Donald Meyers is sick in bed?"

"Scarlet fever?"

"The doctor hasn't said that it is scarlet fever—at least he hasn't put up a quarantine sign.

But nobody is allowed to go into or out of the house."

"Poor Red," I murmured, sorry for my chum.

Here the other fellows whistled to me, so I ran into the street. They were talking about the sick one.

"It doesn't seem right," said Scoop, "not to have Red with us."

"He's ornery," grunted Peg, "but when he isn't around you miss him."

Hurrying, we shortly came within sight of the whispering pines. On the moment they looked fearfully grim and spooky to me. I shivered a bit as I followed my chums up the path.

It came ten-eleven-twelve o'clock.

"Midnight!" grinned Peg. "Now listen for the ghost."

I held my breath. In the deep silence I could hear the rubbing of my fidgety fingers. Then from without the kitchen door came a faint pat! pat! pat! Some one was crossing the porch on tiptoes. The doorknob turned—slowly, with scarcely a sound.

Gosh! I don't mind telling you that I was scared stiff.

"The spy!" breathed Scoop.

Five-ten minutes passed.

"He heard us in here," said Tom, "and beat it."

Evidently this was the case. For the outside world within range of our ears was a well of silence into daybreak.

Tom got breakfast. And when the dishes were washed and put away, we went outside and covered every inch of the yard. But the midnight prowler had dropped no clews.

We had dinner; then we played games in the front yard. Darkness came. And again we heard the mysterious prowler on the back porch. But this was the night's only disturbance.

Scoop, I noticed, was pressing hard on his thinker.

"If ever there was a time when I wanted to skip school," he said to us at breakfast, "it's to-day."

I knew what was worrying him. He was afraid that while we were in school the spy would break into the unguarded house and dig up the talking frog.

Yes, it was risky leaving the frog in the house without a guard. We talked it over.

"If you don't want to leave the frog here," I said to our leader, "why don't you carry it along with you to school?"

"It won't go in my pocket."

"Put it in a lunch box. You can keep the lunch box in your desk. Miss Grimes won't know what you've got in it. She'll think it's full of sandwiches and pickles."

Miss Grimes is our teacher. I suppose she's all right. But I don't like her. She's too cranky.

We went to the cellar and dug up the talking frog. But before we put it in the lunch box that Tom had provided we wound it up and turned the small knobs the way we had seen Mr. Ricks do.

"Hello!" said Scoop, grinning into the tin face.

Nothing happened. He tried it again; then gave the frog a shake.

"R-r-r-r!" rumbled the frog, waking up, sort of.

"Let me do it," I cried, pushing the others aside. Getting my mouth down close, I yelled:

"Rats!"

"R-r-r-a-s!" said the frog.

"Why," said Tom, excited-like, "that's the best it ever did."

"Maybe," I said, with a snicker, "if we jiggle it some more it will talk perfect."

"Nothing like experimenting," grinned Scoop, and he gave the frog another shake.

"*Rats!*" he yelled.

"R-r-r-a-t-s!" rumbled the frog. "R-r-r-a-t-s! R-r-r-a-t-s!"

Scoop laughed.

"Wait a minute; wait a minute," he said, trying to hush the frog up. "You're talking out of your turn. You mustn't say it more than once."

"R-r-r-a-t-s!" rumbled the frog. "R-r-r-a-t-s! R-r-r-a-t-s!"

We pretty near died, we laughed so hard. Then the school bell rang and we dumped the invention into the lunch box and started on the run for the schoolhouse. And every time we jiggled the lunch box the frog would rumble at us: "R-r-r-a-t-s! R-r-r-a-t-s!"

"To-night," grinned Scoop, "we'll try it out on some hard words like 'cat' and 'bat.'"

I had to stay in at recess that morning. For there was a music memory test and, as usual, I got the names of the pieces all mixed up. I'm no good at music.

Maybe all public schools haven't music memory contests, so I'll write down what it is. You see, each room has a talking machine. And at the beginning of the school year the board of education picks out twenty or thirty records. Not easy pieces like, "Yes, We Have No Bananas," but a lot of hard truck that is called *classical.* These records are played over and over again by the teacher. And at the end of the school year we are supposed to be able to write down all of the names of the pieces when the teacher plays them and give the names of the musicians who made them up. . . . It's all right for a fellow who has an ear for music.

"Now," Miss Grimes told me at recess, shoving some records at me, "here are the first four pieces. Take them, one at a time, and play each one over and over again till you know it." Then she went out of the room, closing the door behind her.

It was fun at first. But I got sick of it. The old pieces were no good. So I hunted up something snappy. A band piece with a lot of loud toots in it. And at the first toot, what do you know if the tin frog didn't come to life! "R-r-r-a-t-s!" it rumbled in Scoop's desk, sort of muffled-like. Then the record gave another loud toot and the frog sassed it back. Say, it was bully! There is some sense to that kind of music.

I took the frog out of the lunch box and put it on a chair in front of the talking machine. Mr. Ricks had told us that it was the sound waves that tripped the machinery inside of the frog. I don't understand about sound waves. But I saw right off that it was the loud toots that did the business. And I decided to do some experimenting.

Our talking machine has a cloth front where the music comes out. But one day Bid Stricker skidded and rammed his elbow through the cloth, breaking the bracketwork. And now I discovered that by making a slightly larger hole in the cloth I could squeeze the frog inside.

This worked fine. And I was having a high old time when the door opened and in came Miss Grimes. I thought I'd catch it. But she was complaining to another teacher about something and didn't notice what I was up to. Then the bell rang and the kids all came in.

When school was called, Miss Grimes said to me:

"How many times did you play 'The Maiden's Prayer'?"

"Six times," I guessed, wondering which one of the pieces was that.

"And are you sure that you will recognize it the next time that you hear it?"

"Yes, ma'am," I said, getting fidgety. What worried me was the talking frog. It was still shut up in the talking machine. I was afraid that something would happen.

So I was glad when a knock sounded on the door. And who should come walking into the schoolroom but old Deacon Pillpopper, the man who invented the big community incubator that I told about in my first book, JERRY TODD AND THE WHISPERING MUMMY. If you have read this book you will remember that the Strickers locked me in the incubator, making me think, through a trick note, that the stolen mummy was there. But I got even with them in the end!

We like the friendly deacon. For he's kind of queer. He makes up riddles and puzzles and on his visits to the school he springs the riddles on us, often giving us money if we guess the answers.

Miss Grimes was very polite to the visitor, for he is a member of the county board or something. And directly after reading class she gave him a chance to show off.

"I can see, Mr. Pillpopper," said she, smiling at the old gentleman, "that the boys and girls are all on edge wondering if you have a few new riddles."

And the deacon looked awfully pleased with himself, like a purring cat, sort of, and said:

"Um. . . . Kin I use your blackboard, Miss Grimes?"

And she said:

"Of course, Mr. Pillpopper; of course."

He went to the blackboard and drew a picture and said:

"The moon's got two eyes [he put in the eyes] a nose [he put in the nose] and a big, round face," and he drew a circle around the eyes and the nose. Then he turned and squinted at us. "I've got a dime," he said, "fur the first b'y who kin do that jest like I done it."

Well, every kid in the room shot up his hand to get first chance; and the lucky one went to the blackboard and drew the moon's face and turned to the deacon to thank him for the dime. But the old man chuckled and shook his head. Then another kid tried it. And *he* didn't do it right. Every boy in the room tried it but me. Whatever the trick was, no one caught on to it. I figured I'd be just as unlucky as the rest. But I drew the eyes and the nose and the circle as best I could. And what do you know if the deacon didn't hand me the dime! I pretty near fainted, I was so surprised.

"You see," he told the others, patting me on the head, "Jerry is the only b'y in the room who used his eyes an' noticed that I done it with my *left* hand."

"But he's left-handed," Bid Stricker cried, mad as hops to think that I had won the dime.

At this the deacon scratched his head and looked kind of silly.

He had another test for the girls; and when this was over, Miss Grimes motioned to Amelia Didman to play a few pieces on the talking machine. Amelia got the machine wound up and put the needle down. A familiar toot jumped at me out of the hole in the cloth. And right off I knew that I was in for trouble.

If you can imagine the talking machine record and the tin frog fighting each other tooth and nail, that is how it sounded. First the record would sort of swell up and give an angry toot, as though it was determined to make the frog back up and shut up. And then the frog would dig in and screech: "R-r-r-a-t-s!" And that would make the record madder than ever and it would stomp its front feet like a fighting bull and give a still louder toot. And then the frog would lift itself onto its toes and sass the other. Then they would clinch and knock out each other's false teeth and kick each other in the seat of the pants.

The scholars were laughing fit to kill. Sort of

dazed at first, Miss Grimes' face got red and she hurried to the talking machine to see what was wrong. Then she gave an awful jump. For, as she leaned over the machine, the record and the frog got a strangle hold on each other. *Thump!* The record smashed the frog on the left ear. And when the frog quit wabbling it gave the other a wallop on the snout.

Being a member of the county board, the deacon tried awful hard to be dignified and set a good example and not laugh. But when the record got a smash on the snout that was too much for the old gentleman. He busted right out. And you could hear him cackling above everybody else.

"I guess," said Miss Grimes, frosty-like, "that our talking machine needs repairing," and she shut it off and rapped for order.

As I say, I had expected that I would catch it. But for once I was lucky. And that noon Scoop and I and Tom waited around till the teachers came out of the schoolhouse, then we slipped into the schoolroom and got the frog. I suspect that it is a wonder to Miss Grimes to this day what made her talking machine act up. For when the man came to fix it, he could find nothing wrong with it except the hole in the cloth.

We didn't take the frog to school that afternoon. We put it back in the wooden box and buried the box in the cellar. For Scoop was convinced that to leave it unguarded in the cellar was less of a risk than taking it to school.

CHAPTER V

BUBBLES OF BEAUTY

WEDNESDAY morning when we came into the school grounds a number of the kids were yipping and kicking up their heels. Tom was the first one in our gang to grab the good news that was going around among the scholars.

"Hot dog!" he cried. "Teachers' convention. No school till next Monday."

We were excited. And right away we began to plan our fun.

"Let's catch frogs," suggested Scoop. "We can sell them and make some money. For almost everybody likes fried frog legs."

So we got a bag and started out. First we tried our luck in the millpond behind the brick house. But what frogs we saw there were small and not worth catching. So we decided to go to the ravine where Scoop and I had played dinosaur.

"Risky," said Peg, reflective-like.

"What's risky?" inquired Scoop.

"Leaving the talking frog without a guard."

"You're right," considered Scoop. He fished some matches out of his pocket. "We'll draw cuts," he said, getting the matches ready. "The short-match drawer will be the guard."

"That's fair enough," said Tom, drawing.

I drew next, hoping that I would be lucky. I didn't want to miss the fun of going to the ravine.

Peg got the short match.

"I almost wish," he said, making a wry face, "that I had kept my mouth shut."

Scoop laughed.

"We'll be back by twelve o'clock. So be sure and have dinner ready for us and don't burn the coffee."

We started off, three abreast. But we hadn't gone very far along the country road before we came to a horse and buggy, drawn up in the shade of a high hedge. It was the ricketiest buggy I ever set eyes on. The wheels were warped out of true. They made the buggy look as though it had a bad case of bowlegs. The leather top was cracked and shrunken out of shape.

And the horse! Good night! That horse was so skinny that you could have used its ribs for a washboard. It was sway-backed and its hip bones stuck up like chair knobs. It had a big head, and when I got a look into its sober, forlorn-looking face, I had the uncomfortable feeling that it was dying of a broken heart. I don't know how old horses get to be as a rule. But if some horses live to be fifty years old, this skate was easily sixty-something.

An oldish man was seated in the dilapidated buggy. He had some kind of an iron jigger in his lap. And when he saw us he gave a start, as though he had been caught doing something that he didn't want us to know about. Kerplunk! Quick as scat the iron thing disappeared under the buggy seat.

He was every bit as queer-looking as his old nag. Yes, sir, they were a good pair. The long face that he had turned to us was thin, like a sunfish. The eyes were black, sort of restless-like, and set close together. The head was bald on top. We could see that it was because the man's hat was parked on the buggy seat. He wasn't fat. But he had more stomach than he needed. The way it stuck out in front, like a halved pumpkin, made me think of a lean boa constrictor that had swallowed a dog.

Well, we kind of stared at him, wondering who he was, and he, in turn, squinted back at us.

"Howdy, boys," he smiled, friendly-like.

"Howdy," Tom returned.

It struck me on the moment that my new chum's voice sounded queer. I wondered why. Turning to look at him, to read his thoughts, I found him squinting hard at the old nag. As though he had seen it before and was trying to puzzle out something in his head.

"You boys must be out coonin' chickens," the stranger cackled, pointing to the bag that I was carrying.

"No," I spoke up. "We're planning to fill our bag with frogs."

"Frogs?" he repeated, looking at me questioning-like.

"We're going to sell the hind legs," I explained, "and earn some money."

"Um. . . . How would you like to work fur me? The three of you. Calc'late you kin make a lot more money assistin' me than you kin sellin' frog legs. I've got a real proposition, boys."

"What's your line?" I grinned, looking at the four-legged washboard. "Horse trading?"

I was a little bit suspicious of this stranger. For one time an old shyster came to Tutter and stung me for a dollar and a quarter for a membership in his fake detective agency. Since then

I have been cautious about taking up with men I'm not acquainted with.

Very gravely the old man reached under the buggy seat and brought out a fancy sign. He hung the sign on the side of the buggy. It read:

BUBBLES OF BEAUTY
The Wonder Soap That
Makes All
Women Beautiful

I had heard of Ivory soap and Palmolive soap and two or three other kinds of advertised toilet soap. But I never had heard of Bubbles of Beauty. It must be something brand new, I figured.

The man stood up in the buggy and kind of posed, one hand resting on his over-size stomach and the other feeling around in the air above his head. He looked awfully tall. With his lanky arms and legs and thin face and pushed-out stomach he seemed to be all out of proportion. Looking at him, I was reminded of the funny pictures in the Sunday newspapers.

"Boys," he said, dramatic-like, "I ask you as a disinterested friend, who has done the most for this country, Edison or Gallywiggle?"

I grinned.

"Henry Ford," the old man questioned further, acting as though he was preaching a sermon, "or Gallywiggle?"

Amused, I wondered who Gallywiggle was. I had heard of Mr. Edison and Mr. Ford, but I never had heard of a Mr. Gallywiggle. Gallywiggle! Wasn't that a name for you?

"Mr. Gallywiggle," the old man went on, sort of warming up, "Mr. Mortimor Hackadorne Gallywiggle, the president of our company an' the friend of all humanity. The genius who has taken more warts from women's noses than all of the talkin' machines an' all of the automobiles put together. The man who has made millions of sallow skins pink. The man who has turned bushels of blemishes into barrels of blushes. The man, folks, who spent fifty years of his noble, useful life perfectin' the formula of the greatest gift that science has ever bestowed upon womankind. Bubbles of Beauty! The only toilet soap of its kind in the world. An' to-night, ladies and gents, to introduce this marvelous beautifier into your homes—for one evening, folks, as a special introductory offer—we are cuttin' the price of this household necessity down to only a dime, ten cents, a cake."

"YOUR PROFIT IS A DIME OUT OF EVERY QUARTER!"
SAID THE SOAP MAN.

Suddenly his voice trailed away. And he looked sort of embarrassed-like. I guess he had forgotten himself. I figured it out that he was a soap peddler and was used to talking this way to street-corner crowds.

"Boys," he said, holding our eyes with his own, "if you'll work fur me I'll make you assistant beautifiers. I need you in my business. For this thing of makin' women beautiful is a big job. To do it thorough, like our dear departed president, Mr. Gallywiggle, asked me to do, personal, when he signed my territorial contract, I've got to have plenty of capable help. Mebby you kin guess how turrible I'd feel to learn that I had passed up some poor, unfortunate woman who wanted to be beautiful an' who was left homely simply because I was so rushed that I didn't git around to her with a cake of our marvelous Bubbles of Beauty."

There was a worn black leather satchel in the buggy. He opened this satchel and took out several small cardboard boxes. Removing the cover of one of the pink boxes, he let us see that it contained three thin cakes of soap. It was swell soap all right. I could tell by the smell.

"As I started to say," the soap man continued, "my name is Ajax Posselwait. I'm on a' advertisin' tour through this section of the country gittin' folks acquainted with our marvelous Bubbles of Beauty, the wonder soap that makes all women beautiful. To introduce the soap into every home we are offerin' three cakes for a quarter. In the cities, where thousands of women, yes, millions of women, are usin' Bubbles of Beauty to keep beautiful with, the reg'lar price is fifty cents. But it's all a part of our sellin' plan to put up with a loss in gittin' established in a new territory. We just charge up the loss to advertisin'."

He cleared his throat.

"Now, it ain't goin' to be no trick at all fur you boys, as assistant beautifiers, to sell a box of our marvelous Bubbles of Beauty into every home in this community. All you've got to do is to tell the women how the soap improves the complexion, drives away blotches, transforms wrinkles into dimples. An' fur every quarter that you take in you keep ten cents, which is your pay, an' I git fifteen cents."

I looked at our leader. He had suggested catching frogs as a possible way of earning money. And on the moment it seemed to me that selling this man's soap was a better money-making scheme than frog-catching. He couldn't gyp us, like the fake detective did, because we wouldn't be putting up any money. We were safe.

"Um. . ." said Scoop, thinking.

"You kin make a lot of money workin' fur me," the soap man put in, persuasive-like.

"Maybe," said Scoop.

"It ain't ordinary peddlin'," the man went on. "It's what I call *artistic* peddlin'. Yes, sir, an assistant beautifier must be an artist to be a success at his job. Absolutely. He's got to have enough tact to sell somethin' to a homely woman to make her beautiful without makin' her feel that he knows that she's homely an' needs what she's buyin' from him. Doin' a thing like that successfully is an art, just the same as paintin' beautiful pictures an' carvin' statues. It's a job that any boy kin be proud of. Fur it calls fur *ability*. An', like I say, your profit is a dime out of every quarter."

"Fifteen cents," said Scoop, whose father is one of the shrewdest business men in Tutter.

"Ten cents," said the soap man, scowling.

"Not enough," said Scoop. He took my arm and started off. "Come on, gang," he said. I tried to hold back, but he hissed in my ear to follow him and keep still. He had a scheme, he said.

"Um. . . . Just wait a minute," the soap man called after us.

We paused and looked back.

"Fifteen cents," said Scoop.

The older one's scowl deepened.

"Plain robbery, that's what! Calc'late though I've got to stand fur it."

Scoop gave me a dig in the ribs with his elbow.

"Fifteen cents," he whispered in my ear, "is better than ten cents. I figured that we could hook him for the extra nickel."

We went to the buggy and our new employer gave each of us four boxes of soap, twelve boxes in all. "Bubbles of Beauty" was printed on the covers in gold lettering.

"You ought to have it all sold by noon," he said.

"Where'll we find you when we want to settle up?" inquired Scoop.

"You boys live in Tutter, I take it."

Our leader nodded.

"As you go into town on this road," the man pointed, "there's a big red brick house on the right-hand side with a yardful of pine trees."

"We know the place," Scoop said quickly, giving Tom and me a look that was intended to shut us up if we had any thought of saying anything.

"Back of the brick house there's a' old mill."

"Yes," said Scoop.

"Well," said the soap man, flapping the lines, "when you want to settle up with me that's where you'll find me."

"In the old mill?"

"Exactly. Git up, Romeo."

CHAPTER VI

THE MYSTERIOUS SOAP MAN

We watched the rickety buggy until it had disappeared in the direction of town in a cloud of dust.

Tom was the first one to speak up.

"I was asleep at the switch," he said, talking more to himself than to us, "not to have suspected it."

Scoop turned quickly.

"Not to have suspected what?" he inquired.

"Last Friday noon," our new chum told us, "that man came to our back door peddling books. And that same night some one tried to steal the talking frog. Don't you see the connection, fellows? The soap man is a spy of Gennor's. That's why he's hanging around here, peddling books one week and soap the next. His peddling is just a blind."

We were excited.

"For almost two weeks," Tom told us, "the

sway-backed horse has been stabled in the deserted mill. I saw it there and wondered whose animal it was. But I never connected it with the book agent or suspected that its owner, a spy of the enemy's, was hiding in the upper part of the mill, watching our house."

Scoop was thinking.

"Posselwait," he murmured, repeating the soap man's name. "Ajax Posselwait. Um. . . ." He started down the road under a sudden idea. "Come on, fellows," he grinned. "We'll go over to Mrs. Kelly's house and sell her some Bubbles of Beauty."

I laughed when he said that. For Mrs. Kelly, who lives in the country, is one of the plainest-looking women you can imagine. She has a fat, freckled face and red hair. Her husband, an old friend of Dad's, was killed in a runaway the year I started to school.

"Do you think you can make her beautiful?" I inquired, grinning at our leader.

"I can't see how we can possibly fail," he laughed, "with such wonderful soap to use on her as this." He squinted into one of his pink boxes and smelled of its contents. Then he added, serious: "Selling her beauty soap, though, is the least important part of our errand. What I want more than her money is a chance to peep into the old Matson Bible."

This recalled to my mind that the murdered puzzle maker and Mrs. Kelly had been related, which explains how the family Bible had come into her possession, together with a number of other things that had belonged to the old man.

"What do you want to read her Bible for?" I inquired, puzzled to understand our leader's motive.

"Well," he countered, "if the miser had a brother, there would be a record of it in the family Bible, wouldn't there?"

"A brother?" I repeated.

"Jerry, didn't you notice anything familiar about the soap peddler?"

"No," I said.

"Then you better have your eyes tested," grunted Scoop. "For he looks a lot like old Mr. Matson. The same thin face; eyes set close together. Don't you remember how the old puzzle maker looked?"

I did remember, for the miser had been dead but two years. And now that Scoop had directed my thoughts to it, I could acknowledge to a distinct resemblance between the soap peddler and the dead man. Certainly, I checked off in my mind, the two men had the same kind of shifting, close-set eyes.

"But the soap man's name is Posselwait," I said, bewildered.

"It's no trick," said Scoop, "for a man engaged in crooked work, as this man is, to change his name."

"You think his real name is Matson?"

"It isn't impossible. Certainly he looks enough like the dead puzzle maker to be his brother."

"Why do you call the murdered man a puzzle maker?" Tom spoke up.

"Because," informed Scoop, "puzzle making was his hobby. A queer old duck, he liked to stump people with original conundrums and puzzles. He was smart about it, too. Just before he was murdered he made a ten-ring wire puzzle that no one could solve but himself. Pa tried it. So did Jerry's pa and half of the men in our town. It was *some* puzzle, I want to tell you! After the old man had been murdered, people tried to find the ten-ring puzzle. But it had disappeared along with the old man's money. And it hasn't been seen or heard of to this day."

"Maybe," said Tom, using his thinker, "the puzzle had something to do with the murder."

Scoop stared, his jaw sagging.

"Why! . . . No one ever thought of that!"

"Queer," I spoke up, still bewildered, "that the murdered man's brother should be a spy of the Chicago manufacturer's. Maybe we're mixed up on that point."

"Not on your life," waggled Tom. "I *know* that the soap man is a spy. For if he isn't, why should he be hiding in the old mill?"

I shrugged.

"Search me," I said.

"His main reason for being in the neighborhood," Tom went on, sure of himself, "isn't to make women beautiful. Not so you can notice it! The spiel he gave us about his wonderful soap was bunk, and nothing else but. He can't string me. For *I* know that it takes more than soap to drive away warts and things. His soap may be good, but it won't do all of the wonderful things that he claims for it."

Scoop grinned.

"We can find out how good the soap is by using it on Mrs. Kelly."

"If it makes *her* beautiful," I laughed, "we ought to get a dollar a cake for it."

"Easy," waggled Scoop, his eyes dancing.

He screwed up his forehead.

"Fellows, it doesn't make any difference to us

whether the soap will make women beautiful or not. We're going to peddle it just the same. For we've got to keep an eye on the soap peddler until we get word from Washington and know for sure that the talking frog drawings have been registered and that everything is safe for us. By working for mister spy as assistant beautifiers, we will be able to camp on his trail and no questions asked. See?"

There was sense in that all right.

On our way to Mrs. Kelly's house we came to the Pederson farm. Mr. and Mrs. Orvil Pederson are Norwegians. When they talk English they get their words twisted up.

"Well," I grinned, "if we're going to do any beautifying this morning, we might as well start in here."

"Sure thing," laughed Scoop. He patted me on the back. "You're a good talker, Jerry. Go ahead and show your stuff."

The other fellows followed me to the porch and I knocked, chesty-like, on the kitchen door. Mrs. Pederson was cooking something that smelled awfully good. It was a warm September day. When she came to the door her face was two shades redder than a ripe tomato. Her nose was red, too. She didn't look very beautiful.

Taking a cake of Bubbles of Beauty from a box, I began:

"Mrs. Pederson, your face tells me that you haven't been using the right kind of toilet soap." I showed her the cake in my hand. "This kind of soap," I told her, "will make you beautiful."

"What?" she cried, in a shrill voice. "Is it so ugly that I am in my face that you should come here to tell me about it in my own house like a young smart aleck?"

I saw that I had made a bad start.

"I mean," I said quickly, "that you will become even more beautiful than you are if you will use our marvelous Bubbles of Beauty instead of just ordinary toilet soap. Bubbles of Beauty," I recited, "has taken more warts from women's noses than all of the automobiles and talking machines in the world. It changes wrinkles into dimples; blemishes into blushes; makes sallow skins pink."

You see, I have a good memory!

"Mrs. Pederson," I went on, getting in some of the soap man's gestures as I recited his street-corner speech, "let me ask you as a disinterested friend, who has done the most for this country, Mr. Edison or Mr. Pollywiggle?"

"*Gally*wiggle," Scoop hissed into my ear.

"Mr. Ford," I went on, "or Mr. Gallywiggle?"

My customer blinked her eyes and looked dizzy.

"Mr. Mortimor Hackadorne Gallywiggle," I recited, using my hands, "the president of our company, the friend of all human beings. The man who has turned bushels of blemishes into barrels of—of——"

"Blushes," prompted Scoop, and I could hear him giggling.

Mrs. Pederson opened the door. I thought that she wanted to take a close look at my soap. So I held it out to her, telling her how it took Mr. Gallywiggle, the friend of humanity, fifty years to learn how to make. I told her how wonderfully beautiful she would be when she had used the new toilet soap for a few days. I told her a lot of things. I guess I told her too much!

Swish! Bang! Down came a broom on my head. It made me see seventeen million stars. I was too dazed in the moment and too surprised to run away. I was too dazed even to understand what she was screeching at me as she jabbed me in the stomach with the broom. Scoop saved my life by dragging me down the porch steps.

When I got my senses back, sort of, I was standing in the middle of the country road.

"Anything knocked out of kilter, Jerry?" Scoop inquired, grinning.

"I'm about two inches shorter," I said, feeling of my neck and kind of screwing my head around.

"She gave you some awful wallops."

I admitted it.

"She had no right to do it," Scoop went on, his face darkening. "It wasn't fair. She might have been ladylike and told you to go away if she wasn't interested in your soap. Your ma and my ma wouldn't have done a trick like that. No ladylike woman would. . . . She needs a good lesson," he waggled.

"Go up to the door and scold her," laughed Tom.

"Better than that," said Scoop, "I'm going to turn the tables on her and make her coax me to sell her a cake of my soap."

I had a picture of him doing that!

"If you try it," I said, "you better make out your will before you start in."

He grinned at me.

"Jerry, ol' pal, I don't want to hurt your feelings or knock on your system, but I've got a hunch that your selling spiel needs polishing up. It's—— Well, to use the soap peddler's expression, it isn't *artistic*. It lacks tact."

That made me hot.

"I hope that she doesn't get rheumatism in her arms," I shot at him, "when she starts after you with her broom."

I watched him saunter down the farmhouse lane. Then I sat down on a big rock and waited for Mrs. Goliath to get into high gear with her broom. My head hurt something fierce. But I grinned, notwithstanding. Oh, boy, how I grinned! He'd catch it. I was glad. For he was acting altogether too chesty. He needed taking down a peg or two.

CHAPTER VII

WHAT SCOOP DID

I IMAGINED that I could feel the bump on my head getting bigger and bigger as I sat on the rock with my cap in my lap and my four boxes of Mr. Gallywiggle's beauty soap in my cap.

And when I thought of how the bump came to be there, so big and painful, I said to myself, in just anger over Mrs. Pederson's unwarranted attack, that I hoped that she would get her pay for banging me up.

For one thing, I hoped that she would become homelier and homelier. She could become as homely as an old mud fence and I wouldn't let her have a single cake of my beauty soap. No, I wouldn't! She could stay homely for the next million years for all I cared. I'd let some other woman have my soap to get beautiful with—some deserving woman who was kind to boys and used them in the way that boys should be used—good boys, I mean, like myself.

Then I quit grouching in my mind, sort of, to

SWISH! BANG! DOWN CAME A BROOM ON MY HEAD.

Jerry Todd and the Talking Frog. *Page* 59

watch Scoop. He was close to the farmhouse porch, where Mrs. Pederson was still standing, broom in hand. I didn't want to miss the fun of seeing her land on him. Pretty soon, I told myself, he would be yelping for help. I grinned, forgetful of my bump, in the thought of it.

"Good morning, Mrs. Pederson," I heard him say. My, he was polite! His voice was all honey and cream. I got up and went closer.

There was a flower bed beside the porch. He let on as though he was awfully surprised and tickled to find the flower bed there. From his actions you would have thought that a flower bed—*this* flower bed—was the most wonderful and the most important thing in the world.

He ran over and got down on his knees and began touching the flowers as though he was in love with them. He stuck out his nose and smelled of the blossoms with his eyes squinting into the sky. I could imagine from the expression on his face that he was seeing angels. But when I looked up all that I saw was a crow.

"Such beau-utiful geraniums," he gurgled, letting the word "beautiful" sort of string out, as though it was hard for him to bite off some of the letters. "My," he said, "it must take a lot of skill and a lot of patience to raise such beau-utiful flowers. Ma says it's a knack. *She* can't raise sunflowers, hardly. Isn't this a Martha Washington?"

"Um. . ." said Mrs. Pederson, thawing out, sort of.

"And I do declare!" Scoop gurgled, acting as though he had just discovered a diamond mine. "If here isn't a rose geranium—a *perfect* specimen. Why, it's got four buds on it! And just look at this blossom!" He raised his eyes. "Mrs. Pederson," he said, sober, "you ought to go into the flower business. Why, the way you can make flowers grow you'd become rich and famous in no time at all."

The flattered owner of the flowers left her broom on the porch and came down the steps. Pretty soon she was on her knees beside the flower bed, jabbering about the flowers as though she was crazy. Scoop was jabbering too. It was very disgusting to me. For I saw what he was up to. He was plastering her with soft soap, to get her dime, and she didn't have sense enough to realize it.

Well, they kept on talking about what a wonderful flower-raiser she was, and how it was a gift, just like writing poetry, only she was doing the most of the talking. Scoop just put in a word now and then to keep her tongue in action.

Pretty soon he removed the covers of his four soap boxes. Counting the cakes of soap, three cakes to a box, he next dumped the cakes onto the grass and counted them. Mrs. Pederson stopped talking to watch him. He counted the cakes a third time. Then he searched his pockets.

"Now," he said to himself, in a worried voice, "doesn't that beat the Dutch?"

"You lose somedings?" inquired Mrs. Pederson, inquisitive-like.

She reached down to pick up one of the cakes of soap, curious, I imagine, to feel of the soap and to smell of it, as I have seen women do in the ten-cent stores. But Scoop quickly held out his hand and headed her off. Then he took his handkerchief and flicked imaginary particles of dust from the soap cake.

"This cake," he told the flower raiser, "is the one that I'm saving for Mrs. Tompkins to look at," and he gave it another careful dusting, squinting at it critical-like, his head cocked on one side. Then he carefully dusted each cake in turn, taking a lot of time. "This one," he pointed out, "I'm saving for Mrs. Morrisy to look at and this one for Mrs. Smith and this one for Mrs. Gronke and this one for——" Well, in short, he named over practically all of the women in the neighborhood, customers of his father's grocery store.

Mrs. Pederson was busting with curiosity. She showed it in her actions. She was thinking to herself, I imagine, that here was something going on in the neighborhood that she didn't know anything about. Probably she felt slighted.

"What 'tis?" she inquired shrilly, a queer eager look in her eyes.

But Scoop was busy counting his soap and gave her no attention.

"I guess," he said, still worried, "that I must have made a mistake. I figured that I had an extra cake for you, Mrs. Pederson. But instead of having twelve cakes, the number that I started out with, I can count only eleven."

The woman squinted eagerly at the cakes of soap that had been spread on the grass in front of her.

"A new kind of soap?" she inquired.

"Bubbles of Beauty," recited Scoop, "the wonder soap that makes all women beautiful. Of course," he added, "to a beautiful woman this soap would be of no more use than a pair of skates would be to an Arab in the Sahara Desert.

But take a plain woman like—er—Mrs. Townsend——"

"Yes," said Mrs. Pederson quickly.

"And Mrs. Morrisy," continued Scoop, naming another woman who lived in the neighborhood.

"Yes."

"Unfortunately," said Scoop, "they aren't beautiful. Still, they want to be beautiful. Every woman does, I imagine. So you can imagine how they will welcome our Bubbles of Beauty. But you mustn't repeat what I am telling you, Mrs. Pederson. Oh, no! For your neighbors would be as mad as hops to have the story get out. They will want to have the source of their sudden beauty kept a secret. Don't you see?"

"Oh, yes," said Mrs. Pederson.

Scoop again searched his pockets.

"It gets me," he said, puzzled, "what I did with that extra cake—the one that I was saving for you." He counted the cakes on the grass. And every time that his finger moved Mrs. Pederson's eyes moved with it. She had her nose so close to the soap that it was a wonder to me that she kept her balance and didn't fall forward on her face.

"I was going to let you have a cake," said Scoop, "but you can see for yourself that I have only enough to go around. Of course," he added quickly, "I realize that you haven't any use for the soap yourself. It's only for women who aren't beautiful. But I thought that you might know of some poor, unfortunate woman who has been homely all her life, with a sallow skin and warts and blemishes and wrinkles and——"

"Yes," cut in Mrs. Pederson.

I began to think that "yes" was all she knew how to say.

"Considering what it does," said Scoop, "the soap is very cheap at ten cents a cake, or three cakes for a quarter. I'm sorry, Mrs. Pederson, that I haven't any extra cakes. I know how disappointed you are. No doubt you are thinking of some unfortunate woman friend who has warts and wrinkles; and, in your kind-hearted way, you would give anything, almost, to be able to send this unfortunate friend a cake of our marvelous Bubbles of Beauty, which has the directions for its proper use printed on the bottom of each box. See, Mrs. Pederson?" and he showed her the printing. "I'll be over this fall," he concluded, "for the geranium slips that you promised me."

He slowly gathered up the soap, patting each cake, sort of, as though it was very dear to his heart. And he smelled of each cake and waved it under Mrs. Pederson's nose so that she could smell of it.

Suddenly he straightened and gave a glad cry.

"Why! . . . I know where my extra cake is." He jerked off his cap and there was the lost cake on top of his head. He must have placed it under his cap while I was sitting on the rock.

Mrs. Pederson reached quickly for the soap.

"It will be ten cents," Scoop told her, stepping back.

She hurried into the house and came out with her pocketbook.

When we were in the road, our leader looked back at the farmhouse and laughed.

"That's the time, Mrs. Pederson," he said, "that *we* came out ahead."

"Why didn't you sell her a couple of boxes?" Tom inquired, disappointed.

But Scoop shook his head.

"No. That wasn't a part of my scheme. As a matter of fact I took an unfair advantage of her in selling her the one cake. I *pretended*. And that isn't good salesmanship. But you know why I did it." He looked at me and grinned. "Cheer up, Jerry. Watch how I do it. Then you'll be more successful next time."

He was acting chesty again. It got under my

skin. A fellow hates to be as unlucky as I was. Mrs. Pederson had whanged me on the head with a broom when *I* had tried to sell her a cake of beauty soap. And *he* had hooked her for a dime, just as easy as pie.

"You talk as though you know a lot about salesmanship," I spit out, wanting to pick on him in my grouch.

"I know," he said, waggling, "that good salesmanship is honest salesmanship. For Pa says so."

"Huh!"

He grinned at me in a tantalizing way.

"Jerry, you might make a good wheelbarrow inspector on a ditching crew—something that doesn't require any skull practice. But you haven't the necessary talent for soap peddling."

"You hate yourself!"

"A thing you don't understand," he added, acting big, "is human nature."

"I don't know how to be an old soft soap slinger, either," I shot at him.

It isn't in me to get mad and stay mad. So pretty soon I got over my grouch. Anyway, I admitted to myself, Scoop, with all of his conceit, was deserving of some praise. For he had turned a neat trick, succeeding where I had failed.

I know how to be fair.

CHAPTER VIII

IN THE OLD MILL

ON the way to Mrs. Kelly's house we stopped at the Gronke farm and talked the housekeeper into buying a box of our beauty soap. At the next farm we sold a box to Mrs. Smith, though it took an awful lot of persuasion. At the third farmhouse we were turned down cold. Our beauty soap, Mrs. Morrisy told us, uninterested, was a fraud.

It was now after eleven o'clock by Scoop's watch.

"We've got to snap into it," he said, "if we expect to get back to town in time for dinner."

So we speeded up. And coming to Mrs. Kelly's house, we passed quickly through the gate and followed the cinder path to the kitchen porch.

But no one came to the door when we rapped.

"Dog-gone!" growled Scoop. "All this walk for nothing."

"Don't overlook the fact," I laughed, "that

we have sold seven cakes of beauty soap. Our time in coming here hasn't been wasted."

"Just the same," said Scoop, "it's a disappointment to me not to find Mrs. Kelly at home. I wanted to see her Bible and ask her some questions. For it's important, I think, to find out all we can about the queer soap man."

There was a short silence in which our leader thought of the money that we had taken in and counted it.

"Sixty cents. We'll stop and settle up with the soap peddler as soon as we get back to town."

"What's the rush?" I inquired. "Why not sell the rest of our soap and then call on him?"

"The oftener we stop and talk with him," said Scoop, in good wisdom, "the more we'll be likely to find out."

The old mill that I have mentioned in my story is a part of the Matson property and is situated directly behind the brick house where Tom lives. In his younger days Mr. Matson used to run the mill himself, grinding wheat and corn and buckwheat for the farmers. But he neglected his business after his wife's death. In consequence his trade dropped off. Then, over a period of years, the mill was still. The machinery rusted and became worthless and the wooden water wheel rotted to pieces. Instead of taking care of his property, as any sensible man should have done, Mr. Matson did nothing but work on puzzles.

Just before the murder the mill was gutted of its worthless machinery. A junk man bought it, I believe. When the machinery had been removed, the stone building's doors and windows were boarded up. Mr. Matson did the job himself. Signs were then posted at the mill's approaches warning the public to keep away. But it wasn't very long before the Tutter kids, including myself and my chums, contrived a way of getting into the forbidden mill. It was a peachy place to play bandit. Then came the murder. We had free run of the mill after that. And to let in more light we took down the most of the boards that had been nailed over the doors and windows.

You will know that Mr. Matson was indeed a queer old man when I tell you that he built an office, a small room with windows on all four sides, in the very top of his mill. To get to it one had to climb two flights of stairs.

Coming into the edge of town, Tom went home to help Peg get dinner while Scoop and I circled to the right to the mill pond. The mill yard was a tangle of weeds and underbrush. Here we found Romeo, the soap man's skinny horse, nibbling at the wilted leaves of a squatty elm tree. The horse gave us a mournful look as we approached, then turned its head away and proceeded sorrowfully with its dinner of elm leaves.

"Poor old nag," murmured Scoop, giving the hungry horse a sympathetic eye. "I'm going to bring it some oats."

Entering the mill, we found the soap man cooking something in a dirty kettle over an old oil stove.

"Howdy, boys," the cook greeted, stirring the bubbling contents of the kettle to keep the stuff from burning.

Scoop jingled the coins in his pants pocket.

"We've come to settle up," he informed.

"Just wait a minute," the old man said quickly. He lifted the kettle to one side, away from the smoking flame, and wiped his sticky hands on his pants. "Got it all sold?" he inquired, and there was a look in his thin face, a gluttonous, hungry look, that made me think of a starving wolf.

"Not all of it," returned Scoop.

The thin face showed disappointment.

"How much did you sell?"

"Two full boxes and a separate cake," informed Scoop. "Here's your twenty cents out of the fifty cents that we got for the two boxes. We'll split the dime fifty-fifty."

"Poor," complained the old man, giving us a dark, dissatisfied look. "Awful poor. Evidently you boys hain't as smart as I took you to be. Fur I figured that you'd sell at least ten boxes."

"Give us time," said Scoop. "We've got to learn how to do it."

"You're goin' to keep on, hey?"

"Of course."

"The other boy, too?"

He meant Tom.

"Sure thing," nodded Scoop. "We're going to work in town this afternoon. We ought to sell twenty-thirty boxes."

Again I was reminded of a wolf by the greedy light in the old man's close-set eyes.

"Good!" he said, licking his lips. "Good!"

Scoop squinted around the big empty room. His eyes took in the heavy overhead beams and the cobwebby stone walls.

"How did you happen to find this place?" he quizzed.

"I'm thinkin' of buyin' it," the old man joked, "an' havin' it remodeled into an apartment buildin'. Don't you think it'd make a swell home fur me?"

"Well," said Scoop, noticing, I guess, that the other hadn't answered his question, "if you decide to live here you'll have some fine neighbors." He pointed to the near-by brick house, visible through the open door. "I suppose you know who lives there."

A queer, dark look flashed into the old man's face. It was there for an instant; then it was gone.

"I hain't interested in inventors," he muttered. He got his black satchel. "How many more boxes of soap be you boys wantin' to take with you?"

"Oh, fifteen or twenty," said Scoop. "Do you sleep here?"

"I've got some blankets upstairs."

"On the third floor?"

The old man nodded.

"That's the office," said Scoop.

"Office?"

"The man who used to own this mill," explained Scoop, "built the little room on the third floor for an office. A queer place for an office. Don't you think so?"

"Here's your soap."

"Are you going to be in town very long?"

"That all depends on how much stuff I sell."

"Soap?"

"Of course. Soap sellin' is my business."

"Why don't you sell books? You'd earn more money."

"Sonny, let me tell you somethin'—keep away from books if you ever start peddlin' on your own hook. Fur they hain't no money in lit'ature. I've tried it, an' I know what I'm talkin' about. . . . Now git."

"You didn't find out very much," I grinned at Scoop when we were outside.

"I found out all that I expected to find out," he returned, satisfied. He looked back at the soap man, who was standing in the mill doorway. "A spy, all right. His face gave him away when I mentioned Mr. Ricks. Didn't you notice, Jerry? And, just as Tom has suspected, he's doing his spying on the brick house from the office windows." There was a moment's pause. "Book peddler—soap peddler—spy," murmured Scoop. "A queer man and a crooked man. We've got to keep our eyes on him."

That afternoon Tom stood guard in the brick house while the rest of us peddled soap, each on a different street.

"How's Red?" I inquired of Mrs. Meyers, when she had come to the front door of her house in response to my ring.

"We're keeping him in bed. But he doesn't seem to be very sick. So with plenty of pie and ice cream," she joked, "we hope to pull him through."

"Has he still got spots on his back?"

She nodded.

"What he needs," I told her, as a quick-minded salesman, "is a cake of our beauty soap."

"Beauty soap?" she repeated.

I held up one of my pink boxes.

"Bubbles of Beauty," I recited, "the wonder soap that makes all women beautiful. It cures warts and blemishes," I added, "so it ought to be good for blotches. Don't you think so?"

She laughed.

"Jerry, where in the world did you get this soap?"

I told her about the old soap man in the deserted mill.

"I've sold six boxes," I bragged.

"To women?"

"Sure thing," I grinned. "You better buy a box, Mrs. Meyers. Of course," I added quickly, "I realize that you don't need it yourself, for you are beautiful already. But you can use it on Red."

"On his back?"

"Well," I laughed, with a picture in my mind of Red's homely face, "it won't do any harm if you use some of it on the roof of his nose. For it's good for freckles."

She bought a box. And when I was making change the Stricker gang came into sight in the street.

"See how pretty he is!" Bid hooted, pointing me out to the other fellows.

"Why shouldn't he be pretty?" Jimmy yipped. "He uses Bubbles of Beauty."

"Beat it," I told Bid, scowling, "or the first thing you know I'll step on you and bend you out of shape."

I met Scoop on the corner. He was grinning and happy.

"How's business, Jerry?"

"Fine and dandy," I told him. "I've sold seven boxes."

"Hot dog!" he cried. "I've sold nine."

"Let's knock off," I suggested, "and call it a day."

We picked up Peg in a candy store on Main Street.

"What do you know, fellows?" he grinned, a jawbreaker in each cheek. "I sold a box of beauty soap to Miss Prindle!"

Maybe you remember Miss Prindle, the Tutter dressmaker. I told about her in my book, JERRY TODD AND THE ROSE-COLORED CAT. She is the woman who owned the crab-apple marmalade that our cats got into. We don't like her. None of the Tutter kids do. She's too cranky. You should hear her go for us if we touch her fence or go in her yard! Wough!

"Does she think," laughed Scoop, "that the soap will make her beautiful?"

"Of course," grinned Peg. "What do you suppose I sold it to her for?—to trim petticoats with?"

We laughed. For it struck us as being funny that Miss Prindle, one of the homeliest women in Tutter, had spent her money for a box of Peg's soap in the hope that it would make her beautiful. She had about as much chance of becoming beautiful as Mr. Ricks' talking frog had of growing whiskers.

Our big chum had sold eight boxes of soap. This gave us a total sale of twenty-four boxes. When we put our money together we had an even six dollars. Two dollars and forty cents of this belonged to the soap man. The balance, three dollars and sixty cents, was ours.

"To-morrow," planned Peg, "we ought to sell at least fifteen dollars' worth."

"We're going to be rich," I laughed, contented in our success.

"Let's look at it the other way," grinned Scoop.

"What do you mean?" I said.

"Think of the good that we are doing. That, my boy," and he put his hand on my head in a fatherly way, "is vastly more important than the money part."

"Scoop, the preacher," laughed Peg.

"Ours," preached Scoop, getting in some of the soap man's fancy gestures, "is a very noble work. We are bringing beauty, and with it happiness, into the starved and discouraged lives of countless sad-hearted, homely women."

"Here," Peg offered, "take this jawbreaker and shut up."

"All the same," I grinned, wanting to help the fun along, "the women who bought our soap are going to be very grateful to us."

"Especially Miss Prindle," said Scoop, sucking on the jawbreaker. "I can imagine how grateful she will be to Peg when she looks into her mirror to-morrow morning and finds a Mary Pickford face smiling back at her."

We were joking of course. We had no idea that the soap would actually make women beautiful. It didn't seem possible.

But it was good soap. We had tried it out. And in selling it we felt that our customers were getting their money's worth, even though they didn't get any beautifying results from its use.

"After supper," Scoop planned, "we'll call at the mill and give the soap man his two dollars and forty cents."

"And get our soap for to-morrow's business," said Peg.

"Exactly."

We stopped at Scoop's barn and got a small bag of oats for Romeo. Then we hurried in the direction of the brick house, where Tom was guarding the talking frog.

We had a lot to tell him.

CHAPTER IX

THE MYSTERY DEEPENS

THE soap man was interesting to me because he was the first spy that I had ever come in contact with. I figured that he must be a sort of detective.

Still, I considered, in the course of my thoughts, he was a queer-looking and a queer-acting detective. Not at all like the detectives that I had read about in stories.

For instance, there was his shabby old horse. What was his object in keeping it? Was it to create the impression, beyond all possible doubt, that he was indeed a poor soap peddler, traveling by horse and buggy from town to town?

As a spy he knew who we were. He knew that we were on Mr. Ricks' side. To him we were the enemy, sort of. Tom especially.

Why, then, had he hired us, out of all the boys in Tutter, to peddle his fake beauty soap? Was he planning to make some secret use of us later on when we were least likely to suspect it?

That was a thing to keep in mind, I concluded, looking out for myself.

Scoop said that we should go ahead and sell all of the soap that we could. There was money in it for us.

"But we'll fool mister spy," he said, "if it's his scheme, in hiring us, to get all of us away from the house at the same time. One of us will always stand guard here to keep him out."

"I locked myself in this afternoon," spoke up Tom.

"That's the stuff," waggled Scoop. "It's better to be safe than sorry."

Having had our supper, we were gathered on the front porch of the brick house. The sun had gone down. It was fast getting dark. And on the moment, as I watched the creeping shadows deepen and lengthen under the eerie pine trees, I wondered uneasily what new adventures the night would unfold for us. I had the feeling, sort of, that we were heading into something risky.

Scoop got up.

"Come on, Jerry," he signaled.

Peg wanted to know where we were going.

"Over to the mill," Scoop informed, "to settle

up with mister spy. You better stay here with Tom. We'll be right back."

Getting Romeo's oats from the back porch, we cut around the barn, Mr. Ricks' workshop, and crawled under a rusty wire fence. We could see the horse in the mill yard. It made a queer gurgling throat sound when we gave it the oats. Poor old nag!

The soap man was nowhere in sight in the lower part of the mill.

"S-h-h-h!" motioned Scoop, tiptoeing across the big empty room. He paused at the foot of the stairs and cupped his hand to his ear.

"Hear anything?" I breathed, at his elbow.

"No. But I bet he's up there."

"Let's call," I suggested, uneasy under the mill's crowding shadows, "and bring him down."

"Why not go up? We may find out something."

"Risky," I said. I looked up the stairs. "See how dark it is."

"Don't be a calf, Jerry. Come on."

Bang!

All of a sudden a hinged board came down of its own weight, striking Scoop, who had taken the lead up the stairs, on the head. And in the same moment a pan clattered to the floor.

I was scared stiff.

"Who's there?" the soap man whispered hollowly down the stairs.

Scoop rubbed his head.

"Why don't you kill a fellow?" he growled.

"Um. . . What are you doin' in here?" came the suspicious inquiry.

"We came to settle up."

"Got some money fur me?"

I could imagine from the speaker's quick inquiry that he was licking his lips. The tone of his voice suggested it.

"I almost wish I hadn't," grumbled Scoop.

"You run into my stair trap," the old man told us, with a kind of smug grin on his thin face, when he had joined us at the foot of the stairs, having lighted his way down with a candle.

I saw right off what he meant. He had fixed a string on the stairs, connected to the hinged board and the balanced pan. In the darkness Scoop had stepped on the string without knowing that it was there, springing the trap and thereby sounding the alarm of our presence in the enemy's territory.

The old man held out his hand, rubbing his thumb and fingers.

"Well," he said, as a hint for us to hurry up and give him his money.

"You must have something up there," said Scoop, pointing up the stairs, "that you don't want us to see."

"What I've got up there," came the quick, sharp response, "you hain't goin' to see. An' if you know what's good fur you, you'll keep away from here nights after this."

He stuck his candle on a beam and counted the money that we gave him. In the flickering light he made a queer picture. There was something about him that gave me the shivers.

What was his secret? What was he doing upstairs that should require him to set a stair trap so that he would be warned of our near-by presence in case we came into the mill?

"I can't let you have any more soap to-night," he told us, when he had finished counting his money. "Fur I hain't got it ready yet. But I'll have it fur you early to-morrow mornin'."

"Do you make it?" quizzed Scoop.

The old man ignored the question.

"Cloudy," he said, squinting out of the door. "Looks a good bit like rain. Good night, boys. An' don't furgit what I told you: This hain't no healthy place fur you to be hangin' around after dark."

Hurrying back to the brick house, we excitedly told our chums about our queer adventure in the old mill.

"We'll separate," planned Scoop, "and work in pairs. That'll be the safest. Peg, you and Tom can stay here and guard the house. Jerry and I will watch the mill. And if the spy comes out, we'll follow him."

"I've had jobs I liked better," I told him, uneasy.

"Keep the doors locked," he instructed the house guards. "If we want to get in, we'll tap on the kitchen window. Like this—see?" and he gave two taps, then one tap, then three taps.

I went with him to the mill, dropping onto my stomach in the weeds just without the mill door. It was good and dark now. But our eyes had become accustomed to the darkness. If the soap man came out of the mill, a moving black shape, we would be sure to see him even if we didn't hear him.

An hour passed. I was beginning to get stiff.

"What was that?" breathed Scoop, clutching my arm.

I hadn't heard anything.

"There!"

I sharpened my ears. Thump! thump! thump! It was a muffled sound. Only by straining my ears could I distinguish it above the ordinary night sounds that came out of the mill-pond marsh.

"It's in the upper part of the mill," whispered Scoop. "Let's go in and find out what it is."

"No!" I cried, in a sudden panic, sort of.

Thump! thump! thump!

Scoop got up and tiptoed to the mill, a few feet away, putting his ear to the thick stone wall.

"Jerry!"

I joined him.

"I can hear it plain," he told me. "Put your ear to the wall."

"What the dickens? . . ." I said, bewildered.

"He's drilling a hole in the stone wall. What we hear is the thump! thump! of his hammer."

He suddenly clutched my arm.

"Down!" he hissed in my ear.

I fell flat.

"What was it?" I breathed, trembling all over.

"There's some one over there by that elm tree. See?"

My heart was making an awful racket.

"Looks like a boy," breathed Scoop, squinting. "Here he comes. He's going into the mill."

Two-three minutes passed.

Bang!

"It's the stair trap," Scoop cried in my ear. "The boy walked into it. Here he comes. On the run. Listen, Jerry! I'm going to follow him. I want to find out who he is. You wait here till I get back."

He was gone before I could speak up.

A light had appeared in the mill. I could hear the soap man grumbling to himself as he came down the stairs. Holding the candle above his head, he pottered to the mill doorway and looked out.

"It's them snoopy kids," he muttered, and his face was dark and threatening in its expression. "I'm goin' to lay it on them with a strap if they don't mind me an' keep away from here."

He went back up the steps, resetting his trap, blowing out the candle when he got to the top floor.

The big clock in the college chapel tower donged ten times. Then, at fifteen-minute intervals, it donged the quarter hours.

Eleven o'clock! Scoop had been gone for more

than an hour. Where was he? Why didn't he come back?

It was moonlight now. And with the cold white light had come a dampness that penetrated my sweater and set me to shivering. I pumped my arms to speed up my blood. I got warm after a few minutes. But I still shivered. It was my nerves.

I stuck it out another half hour. Then I got up, wabbling at first on my cramped, trembling legs. Limping to the brick house, I signaled to Peg and Tom to let me in.

"Who is it?" Peg inquired through the kitchen window.

"Jerry," I told him.

He opened the door for me.

"Where's Scoop?" Tom inquired.

While I was talking, telling my story, the missing one signaled on the window.

"Is Jerry here?" he inquired quickly of Peg, when he was inside.

I stepped into sight.

"I went to the mill to get you," Scoop panted, looking worried. "I was scared when I couldn't find you. Did anything happen to you?"

I shook my head.

"Jerry just came in," Peg explained. "He got

to shivering and couldn't stand it any longer. He was telling us about the boy that you followed. Who was it?"

The panting newcomer dropped wearily into a chair.

"Gosh, I'm tired!" He gave a jerky laugh. "Where do you suppose I've been?"

"Tell us," urged Peg.

"First," I put in, "tell us who the boy was."

Scoop shook his head.

"I don't know, Jerry."

"Didn't you follow him home?" I inquired, disappointed.

"Sure thing."

"Then you ought to know who he is."

"I followed him into the country," said Scoop, "to Mrs. Kelly's house, and watched him crawl in through a window. Once I got pretty close to him, though not close enough to see his face. He seemed to be about your size, Jerry. Had on knee pants. And that's all I can tell you about him."

"I didn't know," Peg spoke up, "that Mrs. Kelly had a boy living with her."

"Neither did I," said Scoop. "That's what puzzles and mystifies me. Who is he? And why did he go to the old mill? It wasn't to see the soap man, or the two would have met and talked together."

Pat! pat! pat!

"The spy!" breathed Tom, listening to the footsteps on the porch.

The doorknob turned. We heard more muffled footsteps. Then silence.

"Go lay down," Peg told Scoop, "and get some sleep. For you look tired out. We'll take care of things while you sleep."

"Just a minute," said Scoop, feeling in his pockets. He brought out a piece of cloth, handing it to me.

"Did you ever see it before, Jerry?"

I took the piece of cloth and squinted at it.

"Why," I said, surprised, "it's the patch that you and Peg sewed on my old corduroy pants."

One time when I was playing at Scoop's house I tore an awful hole in the seat of my pants, a knock-about pair that I wore on Saturdays. Peg was there. And he and Scoop, in fun, took me down and sewed a heart-shaped patch over the hole. They even went to the trouble of putting a red edge on the patch, using some of Mrs. Ellery's fancy darning cotton. I didn't mind their joke. I got just as much fun out of it as they did. Afterwards Mother wanted to rip off the patch and put on something less showy. But I wouldn't let her change it.

"I heard the kid's pants rip," Scoop went on, "when he went through a barbed-wire fence. And when I came to the fence, there was this patch. I thought it was the one that I had helped to sew on Jerry. I wasn't sure though."

Peg scratched his head.

"But how could a strange kid get hold of Jerry's pants?"

"You tell me," said Scoop, wagging his head, "and I'll tell you."

"Are you sure it's your patch?" Peg inquired of me.

I told him that it was, beyond all doubt. And I tried to remember the last time that I had worn the old corduroys. It came to me slowly that I hadn't seen them in my clothes closet for a good many weeks.

How had they come into the possession of this strange boy? Why was he wearing them instead of his own pants? Who was he?

I pondered the mystery, puzzled.

CHAPTER X

A SURPRISE

It was our leader's theory that the spy was a brother of the murdered puzzle maker's. That would make him a relative of Mrs. Kelly's. A mysterious boy, from Mrs. Kelly's house, had been in the old mill where the soap man was living.

What was the connection between Mrs. Kelly and the mysterious boy and the queer old peddler?

Was there a blood relationship between the man and the woman, as Scoop suspected? Were the two working together to some hidden purpose? What was the man doing in the upper part of the mill? Was he drilling a hole in the thick stone wall? Did Mrs. Kelly know what he was doing and why he was doing it? And, in conclusion, was she in league with the spy in his unworthy scheme to steal Mr. Ricks' talking frog?

We had pledged ourselves, as Tom's loyal

chums, to stand by him and help him save the talking frog from thieving hands. And now that Mrs. Kelly had become involved in the tangle, seemingly on the spy's side, it was highly important for us, in our campaign against the enemy, to have an early talk with her, to pump her, and to thus find out if she were related to the soap man. Also we would pump her, Scoop said, to find out who the boy was who was wearing my old corduroy pants.

"The more we learn about the enemy's plans," he told us, when we talked the matter over at the breakfast table, "the better chance we'll have of winning out."

Our plans completed, he and I headed into the country immediately after breakfast, leaving Tom and Peg to wash the dishes and take care of the house.

"Sure," Mrs. Kelly cried, when our knock had brought her to the kitchen door, "it's the Ellery boy and the mayor." She gave me that nickname the time that Dad was elected mayor of Tutter. Opening the screen door, she brushed out some flies with her apron and took my arm. "Come right in," she invited, making a fuss over me. She is that way with everybody. That is why she is so well liked. She frequently comes to our house. Mother buys eggs from her and gives her dresses to make over for herself. She is kind of poor, I guess.

We sat down in the chairs that she brought for us and answered the questions that she asked us about our folks—how well they were and what they were doing. And, of course, she had to tell me what a big boy I was getting to be. She does that every time I see her.

All the time that we were talking, Scoop was squinting around the kitchen. I knew why. In a house where a boy lives one usually expects to see a cap or a shoe or a baseball or something like that laying around on the floor. But there were no boy's things in this room.

"It must be kind of lonesome for you," said my companion, "living here by yourself."

He was starting to pump the other to find out whether she was on our side or the spy's.

"Yes," said Mrs. Kelly.

"I don't suppose," the smooth one followed up, "that you keep a hired man."

"People on three-acre farms," the woman laughed, "don't usually keep hired hands."

"I should think, though," said Scoop, "that a boy would be a big help to you in running your little farm."

"I had a boy last year," said Mrs. Kelly. "But this year I have managed to do the work myself."

It was plain to us that she didn't intend to say anything about the boy who was living with her. So Scoop cleverly shifted the conversation to the murdered puzzle maker.

"It doesn't seem possible," he said, "that old Mr. Matson has been dead three years. How the time flies!"

"Two years," corrected Mrs. Kelly.

"No," said Scoop, acting sure of himself, "he has been dead three years."

Well, they argued back and forth, and finally, to prove that she was right, she brought out the family Bible.

"There," she said, in an I-told-you-so tone of voice, laying the Bible on the kitchen table. " 'Born in 1850; died in 1920.' "

"Where do you see that?" inquired Scoop, putting his nose down close to the page. I knew that he wasn't looking where her finger pointed. Not at all! Having worked her into bringing out the family Bible, the one that the puzzle maker had owned, he was squinting all over the page, taking in everything, births and deaths and marriages.

Finally he straightened.

"You're right, Mrs. Kelly," he waggled, giving in.

The woman beamed in her victory.

"Sure," she said, in her kindly way, "you lads both have a hungry look. Let me bring out my cookie jar," and she bustled into the pantry.

No sooner was she out of sight than Scoop hissed at me:

"There's a twin brother, Jerry. Peter Matson. It's the soap man, all right."

"Jinks!" I said, keeping my eyes on the pantry door.

"The last record on the page is what stumps me."

I could hear Mrs. Kelly coming.

"Yes?" I said, breathing hard.

"'Frances Matson, granddaughter, born 1910,'" recited Scoop. "I never heard of a granddaughter. Did you, Jerry?"

Before I could reply Mrs. Kelly came into the room with a brown jar in her hands.

"Help yourselves," she invited, setting the cookie jar on the table.

I ate ten cookies and Scoop ate eleven. He made a pig of himself I thought.

"We're peddling beauty soap," I told Mrs. Kelly, bringing out a pink box. "The regular price of the soap is ten cents a cake or three cakes for a quarter. But I want you to have a free cake," I told her, "to sort of pay you back for the cookies."

"Beauty soap?" she repeated. And I had the sudden feeling that something queer was happening in her head.

"It's a very wonderful soap," Scoop picked up. "It makes women beautiful. The homelier they are the more beautiful they become. And we have been told further that it removes warts and blemishes; turns wrinkles into dimples. Of course," he said, in pretended earnestness, "I realize that you haven't any use for the soap yourself. But maybe you have a friend who is homely and who wants to become beautiful. And in your kind-hearted way——"

"What is the name of your soap?" Mrs. Kelly cut in.

"Bubbles of Beauty," recited Scoop.

"Here it is," I said, opening my pink box and handing her a cake.

She turned white—a sort of scared-looking, yellowish white, like the keys of an old piano.

"So he's in the neighborhood, is he? The ould scoundrel! When did you meet him? This mornin'?"

"Yesterday morning," informed Scoop.

"And did he send you here?"

"Oh, no," Scoop said quickly.

"Where is he now?"

"In the old Matson mill."

She gave a low cry, as though something pained her on the inside where her heart was.

"Howard," she inquired earnestly, calling Scoop by his given name, "are you a friend of mine?"

"You bet I'm your friend, Mrs. Kelly."

"Will you help me?"

"Tell me what to do," he waggled, "and I'll do it as best I can."

"Me, too," I put in, excited.

It was plain to us now that Mrs. Kelly wasn't on the soap man's side. We were glad.

"I'm in trouble," she told us, a worried look on her face. "And some one that I think a great deal of is in deeper trouble than me. We're likely to be cheated. It's the soap man. Sure," and her eyes flashed, "I know the ould villain! He's Mr. Matson's twin brother. And he's here to git the ould gintleman's money."

"What?" cried Scoop, jumping up. "Money? What money do you mean?"

"For two years I've kept to myself what I

know, wantin' to carry out the ould gintleman's last wishes. And now, at the last moment, the shyster brother turns up! Sure, 'tis enough to drive me crazy."

Scoop was dancing in front of her.

"What do you mean, Mrs. Kelly, in saying that the soap man is here to get old Mr. Matson's money?"

Instead of answering, the disturbed woman went to a door that opened into a back bedroom.

"Come out, Frances," she called in a quiet voice. "These boys are your friends."

Scoop excitedly clutched my arm.

"That's the kid, Jerry," he hissed in my ear.

I suddenly wondered if my chum was crazy. For he had told me that the strange kid was a boy. And here was a girl!

I was told later that I blushed like a beet. Well, I won't deny that. What boy wouldn't blush, let me ask you, to learn suddenly that a girl he never had seen before had been wearing his corduroy pants around the country, leaving telltale patches in barbed-wire fences?

I had good occasion to blush, let me tell you!

CHAPTER XI

THE BIBLE'S SECRET

I WAS introduced to the strange girl. But I don't remember what I said or what she said. For I was sort of confused.

Later on I came to realize how very pretty she was, with laughing black eyes, saucy bobbed curls and pink cheeks. Her name was Frances Matson. Her father, Mrs. Kelly told us, an only child of the puzzle maker's, had quarreled with his parent, the girl's grandfather, and had run away from home when he was nineteen. Since then, over a period of twenty years, nothing had been heard of him until very recently.

"Just before the ould gintleman met with his awful death," the woman went on, "he came here, as though he had a premonition of what was goin' to happen to him, and told me for the first time about the quarrel that had separated him from his son, Harry. He was wholly to blame, he confessed, and cried about it, great, big tears, tellin' me how stubborn he had been and how sorry he was now. He wanted his son to come home again. And he asked me, as his cousin, to write to all of our relatives to learn if any of them knew anything about the missin' one's whereabouts. He hadn't kept track of his relatives, he explained, and didn't know where to write to, himself. Then he mentioned his advanced age. He wasn't likely to live much longer, he said. He had felt himself breakin' down of late. And he gave me a written order so that in case of his sudden death I would have a right to hold his furniture and household goods until his son had been located. He trusted me, he said, and depended on me. I told him, in sympathy, that I would do my best to find his boy for him. He wanted Harry to heir his property, the brick house that he lived in and the ould mill. He had money, too, he told me, hidden away. In the event that his son wasn't found within ten years, the estate was then to be divided among his relatives, but no part of it, he instructed bitterly, not so much as a penny or a pin, was to go to the rascally twin brother, Peter."

The speaker paused to get her breath.

"And he told me in conclusion," she went on, "that I was to preserve the family Bible and let no one have it except his son, least of all the twin brother, who, accordin' to his story, was the blackest black sheep that ever disgraced a respectable family. And no sooner had he said this than a wild look came into his eyes and away he ran, out of the house and down the road, as though Satan himself was hot on his heels. I knew then that the things that I had been thinkin' about him were true: He was the next thing to crazy. A week later I went to town, stoppin' at his house. He didn't answer when I rang the bell. The door was unlocked. I went in . . . the kitchen floor was covered with blood . . ."

"We know about the murder," Scoop spoke up, "and about the vanished body."

Mrs. Kelly composed herself and proceeded:

"Later I went to the judge and showed him my order. He said it was legal. And with his permission I moved everything out here, storin' the stuff in my barn, all except the Bible. Then I started writin' letters. Sure, I wrote more than a hundred letters. I wrote to all my relatives, near and distant, and to many people who weren't in the family, askin' them did they know anything about the lost son. Finally, about a month ago, I got word that Harry was dead. He had married in his twenties, and the young wife was dead too. There was a granddaughter who had been taken to raise by a family named Knobson. Before

I could get around to write to the Knobsons, I got a letter from Frances herself. She had learned through one of her distant relatives that I was huntin' for her pa. And then——" The speaker broke off shortly and turned to the girl. "But I will let Frances finish the story. For she can tell it better than I can."

"I wrote two letters to Mrs. Kelly," the girl picked up, "and she wrote back telling me about my grandfather, who had been dead for nearly two years, and about his hidden money."

"Hidden money?" cried Scoop, excited.

"Mrs. Kelly thinks," the girl told us, "that there is money hidden in my grandfather's old mill. Having gotten her letters to that point, you can imagine how anxious I was to come here. For the money, if it could be found, was mine. But I didn't dare to tell the Knobsons. No, indeed! For they weren't good to me. And I was afraid that if they knew about the money they would come here, too, and take it away from me and keep it. So I ran away from them last week. Since then I've been in hiding."

"But *I* was told," Scoop said, looking puzzled, "that your grandfather's money was stolen."

"It was the general belief," Mrs. Kelly spoke up, "that the ould gintleman was killed for his hoarded money and that the money disappeared from the house along with the body. But I have had an entirely different opinion. What proof was there, I asked myself after the murder, that the money was stolen? None. The ould gintleman had told me that his money was hid. And I drew the sensible conclusion that it was still hid. At one time I thought of goin' to the judge with my story. But I decided not to do that. For I realized that if the story got out that there was money hid in the ould mill, every Tom, Dick and Harry in Tutter would be there searchin' for it. That would never do. It would be best, I concluded, to keep my thoughts to myself until the son had been found. Then he and I could search together for the hidden fortune."

Scoop looked at me.

"We've been wondering why the old soap man was living in the mill. I guess we know now."

"He has a double purpose in being there," I said.

"Sure thing," waggled Scoop. "He intends to stay there until he has found the hidden money. And then he plans to make another clean-up by stealing the talking frog for Gennor."

"Talking frog?" repeated Mrs. Kelly. "What do you mean by that?"

We told about our new chum and about his father's unusual invention.

"Our chum says," Scoop concluded, "that the spy has been living in the mill for the past two weeks."

"He'll get the money!" cried Mrs. Kelly, in sudden alarm.

"It's very evident," waggled Scoop, "that he knows there is money there. For last night we heard him sounding the stone wall. We thought he was drilling a hole in the wall. More probably, though, he was searching for a possible hollow place."

"Let's hope," I said, "that we find the money ahead of him."

Scoop gave the granddaughter a quizzical look.

"Didn't you know that the man was in the mill last night when you were there?"

The girl blushed. I guess she was thinking about my pants.

"How did you know that I was in the mill?" she countered, embarrassed.

"Jerry and I saw you go in. And when you came out I followed you."

"Oh! . . ." said Mrs. Kelly quickly, nodding her head in a knowing way. "So that is why you came here! I've been wonderin'."

Scoop grinned.

"I heard some one in the upper part of the mill," the girl said. "But I didn't know or suspect that it was my wicked uncle." She shivered. "He might have grabbed me in the dark."

Scoop gave her another quizzical look.

"Is it in order," he queried, "for me to ask you why you went there?"

"I wanted to see if I could find out what 'ten and ten' means."

" 'Ten and ten'?" repeated Scoop, staring.

"It's in the Matson Bible," Mrs. Kelly told us. "One day I came across it. Queer, thinks I, squintin' at it. Then it struck me all of a sudden that the ould gintleman, in his love for puzzles, had put it there for a hidden purpose."

" 'Ten and ten,' " mused Scoop.

"Frances thinks," said Mrs. Kelly, "that it's a key to the money's hidin' place. And if she is right, and we can find out what it means, we'll know where to look for the money."

"Hot dog!" cried Scoop. "This is getting exciting."

"I looked all over the first floor of the mill," the girl said, "trying to find something that would measure 'ten and ten' or was marked 'ten and ten.' Failing to get a clew there, I started up the stairs. I stumbled over something. It made an awful racket. Scared, I turned and ran away as fast as I could."

Scoop looked at me and laughed.

"Well, Jerry, we have one less mystery to solve."

"What do you mean?" the girl inquired quickly.

"We've been wondering," grinned Scoop, "who the strange boy was who was running around in Jerry's pants."

"You must have been awfully close to me," blushed the girl, "to have seen how I was dressed."

Scoop laughed again and told her about the patch.

"I thought it would be fun," she explained, "to disguise myself."

"One time we did that," grinned Scoop, referring to our adventure in solving the mystery of the whispering mummy, "and got into a peck of trouble."

Mrs. Kelly looked at me and smiled.

"Didn't you know, Jerry, that your ma gave me your ould corduroy pants to cut up for patches?"

I didn't know it, and I told her so.

Scoop let his forehead go puckered.

" 'Ten and ten,' " he repeated, thinking. He

looked at Mrs. Kelly. "Did you say it's in the Bible?"

The Book was still on the kitchen table. Mrs. Kelly turned to the tenth chapter of Genesis. Under "Chapter" and "X" was a penciled line with the ends turned up at right angles. And the same kind of a mark was under the tenth verse. Like this:

CHAPTER X

10 And the beginning of his kingdom was Babel, and Erech, and Accad, and Calneh, in the land of Shinar.

Mrs. Kelly then turned to Exodus, the Bible's second book. Here the tenth chapter and the tenth verse were marked in the same way.

"First," she told us, "I thought that there was a hidden meanin' to the marked verses. But I could make no sense of it. Then I discovered that it was 'ten and ten' all through the Book. It's the 'ten and ten,' we have concluded, that carries a hidden meanin', and not the marked verses themselves."

" 'Ten and ten,' " murmured Scoop. "It's another one of Mr. Matson's puzzles all right. No doubt about that. He was great on puzzles. Hiding his money and making a puzzle of the hiding place was right in his line." He turned to me. "Remember the ten-ring puzzle, Jerry?"

I nodded.

"He offered ten dollars," Scoop went on, "to anybody who could work the puzzle. But no one earned the money. For no one could work it but himself." The speaker's voice suddenly broke off. And he caught and held my eyes with his own excited ones. "Gee-miny crickets!" he exploded. "Don't you tumble?" and he clutched my arm and almost pinched it off. "Ten rings! Ten dollars! 'Ten and ten!' The puzzle has something to do with the Bible key!"

Maybe you can imagine how excited we were. Oh, boy!

"This afternoon," planned Scoop, "I'm going to call on old Deacon Pillpopper. For he knows a lot about puzzles. In fact he and Mr. Matson worked together on a number of puzzles. Maybe the old man will know about the ten-ring puzzle and what 'ten and ten' means. I hope so. Boy, won't it be fun digging up the hidden money! Do you think we'll get a thousand dollars, Mrs. Kelly?"

"I'd sooner think," said the woman steadily,

"that we'll get *twenty* thousand dollars. For the ould gintleman was rich, let me tell you."

"Wough!" cried Scoop, acting dizzy.

The clock struck ten, reminding us that it was time for us to start back to town.

Mrs. Kelly followed us to the door.

"Beware of the ould shyster, boys. Watch him. And don't go in the mill nights. Sure, it'd break me all up if anything were to happen to either of you, especially Jerry, whose ma has been so good to me."

"Don't you worry about us," Scoop laughed. "The soap man may be a slick old bird, but we've got a few wing-clipping tricks up our sleeves. Eh, Jerry?"

"You said it," I waggled.

Pausing on the porch, Scoop ran his fingers through his hair.

"'Ten and ten.' Um. . . ." He raised his eyes. "If you find out what it means," he said to the two in the doorway, "telephone to us at the brick house. And if we find out anything new we'll telephone to you. In the meantime we'll keep a sharp eye on mister spy. He won't get away from us with the money. Be assured of that. Come on, Jerry."

CHAPTER XII

SO BEAUTIFUL!

"I WONDER," reflected Scoop, when we were on our way home, "if the Chicago manufacturer knows that his spy is putting in the most of his time treasure hunting."

"Why do you say that?" I inquired, trudging abreast of my companion along the dusty country road.

He didn't answer for a moment or two.

"If *I* were Gennor," he said, absorbed in his thoughts, "I'd send another man here or come myself."

"To help the spy?"

"To find out why the spy didn't get busy."

"He *is* busy," I said.

"Treasure hunting—yes. But he wasn't sent here to drill holes in stone walls."

"He probably would get busy in a hurry," I reflected, as we walked along, "if he knew that Mr. Ricks was on his way to Washington."

"Gennor knows it," Scoop said quickly.

"What makes you think so?"

"The dress patterns were stolen from Mr. Ricks on the train. That was the work of another spy. And surely the radio man knows what his spies are doing." There was a moment's pause in our conversation. "Yes, sir," Scoop waggled, "it wouldn't surprise me a bit to have Gennor ship another spy down here to check up on the first one."

I had a sudden worried feeling.

"Evidently," my companion continued, thinking, "the soap man knows that the hidden treasure is his biggest stake. That's why he's giving it his first attention. Um. . . . I wonder how he found out about the hidden money."

"Maybe," I suggested, "he got hold of one of Mrs. Kelly's letters."

"I wonder if he didn't."

We were now within sight of the whispering pine trees and the lonely brick house.

"There goes the mail man," I pointed. "He's stopping at the Ricks' mail box. Let's speed up."

But Scoop was pressing on his thinker and didn't seem to hear me.

"To-night," he said, speaking to himself, sort

of, "we're going to find out," and he gave his head a sharp, decisive bob.

I was instantly uneasy.

"Find out what?" I inquired, regarding him steadily with narrowed eyes.

He raised his face and grinned.

"Have you got a lot of grit, Jerry?"

"That all depends," I returned, on my guard. "What are you planning to do?" was my cautious inquiry. "Hold up a bank?"

"To-night," he said, "you and I are going to visit the old mill."

"That's what *you* say."

"We've got to do it," he waggled.

"It's a nice, easy way to commit suicide."

" 'Ten and ten,' " he mused. "What does it mean? What is the spy doing? Has he found the hidden fortune yet? . . . I wish it was dark."

"Too risky for me," I told him.

"The soap man, of course, won't know that we're there."

"You told the truth," I waggled. "He won't know that I'm there, for I don't intend to be there."

My companion gave me another odd grin.

"What's your scheme?" I inquired, curious.

"Let me give it some more thought," he laughed.

Coming to the Ricks' mail box I fished out a letter that the rural carrier had just delivered.

"Is it from Aunt Polly?" Scoop inquired, squinting over my shoulder.

"It can't be," I said, staring at the Atlanta, Georgia, postmark.

However, the letter *was* from Aunt Polly. And when we had read it, the four of us, and were made to understand the situation, our minds were suddenly depressed. For the absent-minded inventor was lost. He had vanished from Springfield in the time that it had taken Tom's aunt to get there. And now, in possession of certain vague clews, the little old lady was trying desperately to locate her brother in Atlanta.

"If you get word from him, wire me immediately," was the letter's concluding injunction.

Tom turned to us with a burning face.

"Isn't Pa the big dunce!" he cried, his lips trembling with mortification. "I never knew anybody like him." Then he stiffened, sort of proud-like, and his mouth went grim in its expression. "But if you fellows are thinking to yourselves that he's 'soft' in his head, you're dead wrong. It's just his queer way," he concluded.

"Shucks!" said Scoop loyally. "We understand."

Here Tom's forehead clouded over.

"Ding bust it!" he cried. "We aren't safe from Gennor by a long shot. And we won't be until Aunt Polly and Pa are in Washington."

We had dinner. Then Scoop and I and Tom went to the old mill to get our supply of beauty soap.

"Um. . ." scowled our disgruntled employer. "I thought you boys was plannin' to come around early this mornin'?"

"We had other business," said Scoop.

"A half day, I suppose, is better than nothin'. Think you kin sell ten boxes apiece this trip?"

"Easy," said Scoop.

"I'll be lookin' fur you after supper," the old man told us as we started away with our supply of beauty soap. "But come before dark," he instructed sharply.

Scoop squinted back at the old mill, a gaunt, ungainly structure with a flat roof. Then he turned to Tom.

"Have you got a kite?" he inquired.

Our new chum shook his head.

"I'll ask Peg to make one," Scoop decided, and he started back toward the brick house, where the fourth member of our gang was standing guard over the buried talking frog.

Tom and I went ahead, leaving Scoop to his own devices. Pretty soon we came to Miss Prindle's house on Church Street. At sight of her dressmaking sign I grinned.

"It must have been an awful blow to her," I told my companion, "not to have been able to change her homely face."

I had no sooner said this than the front door opened and the dressmaker herself appeared on the porch. She looked up and down the street, nodding to us and smiling.

Gosh! I was struck dumb, sort of. It was her face! I blinked my eyes. I must be dreaming, I told myself.

"Pinch me," I said to Tom.

"What for?"

"I want to see if I'm awake."

"You're awake all right," he laughed.

"Do you see what I see?" I asked him.

"I see a house."

"Is there a woman on the porch of the house that you see?"

"Sure thing."

I took another look at the porch's occupant, a sort of protracted, staring look. It couldn't be

Miss Prindle, I told myself. No. It was some other woman, a very beautiful woman, dressed up in the homely one's clothes.

Still, it looked like Miss Prindle, all but the face.

"Good afternoon," I said, touching my cap.

"Good afternoon," she returned, smiling.

It was Miss Prindle's voice all right. But that face!

"How is Mr. White?" I inquired, to a purpose.

"Mr. White?"

"Your husband," I said glibly. "Is he feeling well to-day?"

"You are confusing me with some other woman," she said. "For my name isn't White. I am Miss Prindle."

For a moment or two I was dizzy.

"I—I didn't recognize you," I fumbled. "You—you look different."

"Oh! Do I?" and she laughed.

"You look very beautiful," I told her.

She made no reply. And when she had gone into the house I drew Tom into a seat on the curb. I had to sit down for a few minutes. For a crazy wabble had come into my knees. It was an awful shock to me, let me tell you, to learn that our beauty soap wasn't a fake as we had suspected.

Then I thought of Red. I wondered if his mother had used any of the beauty soap on him. It was hard for me to imagine my red-headed chum with a beautiful face. I wondered what he would look like without his freckles and his red nose.

I got up, telling Tom that I had to go over to Red's house, and together we hurried down the street. As we came within sight of our freckled chum's home, his mother appeared on the front porch and beckoned to us.

"Donald wants you to come around to the east bedroom window," she told us, when we came into the yard. "He has a surprise for you."

I knew what she meant. She had used some of the beauty soap on Red, and now our formerly freckled chum had a Rudolph Valentino face.

"Hello, fellows," Red called to us from the bedroom window. "Do I look any different to you?"

Did he! The sight of him sickened me, sort of. Not until this moment had I realized how very dear to me his freckles were. Now they were gone! His red nose was gone! He would never be the same to me again. The chum I had loved and traded neckties with had vanished forever. And here in his place was a wax-faced doll.

"You—you don't look like the same kid," I told him.

"It's your beauty soap," he grinned.

"Such wonderful soap," put in Mrs. Meyers, beaming at us. "Can I use it on the cat, Jerry? I thought I'd wait and ask you."

When Tom and I were in the street I opened one of my pink boxes and squinted at its contents sort of reverent-like. And I flushed with shame in the thought that only recently I had regarded this wonder soap—this *miracle* soap—as a fake.

While we were standing there, a familiar pottering figure came into sight in the street. It was the old soap man. He was awfully excited. His eyes bulged and his mouth was open. He was panting, sort of. And his stiff legs were going up and down like a jumping jack's.

"I just got a letter," he heaved, "from a Tutter lady by the name of Mary Prindle." He focused his bulging eyes on us. "Do you know her, boys?"

I nodded.

"Yesterday," I told him, still bewildered, "she was as homely as a warty cabbage; and to-day she looks like Mary Pickford on parade."

"It's my soap," the old man waggled, breathing hard. "My wonder soap. She used it last night, an' now she's goin' in the movies."

Miss Prindle in the movies! I stared at him.

"She says so in her letter. Read it."

I did. Here it is:

> Dear Mr. Posselwait:
>
> I feel in duty bound to tell you what excellent results I have gotten from your wonder soap, Bubbles of Beauty. In just one night your soap has transformed me into a dream of beauty. I am seriously thinking of going into the movies.
>
> Miss Mary Prindle.

One time the Stricker gang wrote us a fake note, signing Miss Prindle's name to it, asking us to drop twelve of our cats into her basement window. That was the time that the cats got into her crab-apple marmalade.

If I hadn't seen the beautified dressmaker with my own eyes, I probably would have suspected that this letter of Mr. Posselwait's was another trick of Bid Stricker's. But I knew that the letter was no fake. For I had seen the transformed one with my own eyes. Tom had seen her, too. It was no case of imagination with us.

"You kin take it along with you," the soap man told us, "an' show it to your customers. It ought to help you make sales. Work hard, boys," and he rubbed his hands together like an old miser.

Tom and I went to a house where I had been turned down the preceding afternoon.

"Well?" Mrs. Larson said sharply, coming to her front door. She didn't act very glad to see me. You could have imagined, from the way she looked at me, that I was an alley cat with a choice assortment of smallpox germs.

"Yesterday," I said, in proper dignity, "you told me that my beauty soap was a fraud. In justice to my goods," I concluded, handing her the letter, "I think you ought to read that."

She took the letter and read it through.

"As you know," I said, getting in my selling talk, "Miss Prindle was not a very beautiful woman before she used our beauty soap. But in just one night Bubbles of Beauty, the wonder soap, has transformed her into a dream of beauty. Of course," I added, in good tact, "I realize that you have no use for the soap yourself. It is only for women who are not beautiful. But you may know of some woman who is homely and who wants to become beautiful. And in your kind-hearted way——"

"Excuse me," she laughed. "I have a cake in the oven," and she closed the door in my face.

We went to another house where I had been turned down. Mrs. Macey took my letter and read it.

"Oh!" she laughed. "This is *so* funny."

"What's the matter with all of the women?" Tom said, puzzled. "Why do they say *'Oh!'* when you show them the letter, and act as though they were gagging on something?"

"Search me," I returned, digging at my hair.

Returning to Church Street, I started Tom in where Peg had left off the preceding afternoon, then hurried back to Main Street, my own territory. I called at all of the houses, the full length of the street, making a number of sales. One of the women that I called on was telephoning in the front hall when I came to the door. I courteously waited until she was through talking, then rang the bell.

Her face broke into smiles when she saw me. And she wanted to know if I were the boy who had Miss Prindle's beauty letter.

"I just heard about it over the 'phone," she explained. "May I see it, please?"

She was called back to the telephone before I could locate the letter in my pocket.

"This is one-seven-one-nine," she said sweetly. "Oh! . . . Is it you, Mrs. Bardan? I didn't recognize your voice. No, really I didn't. What was that? Oh, yes! No, I haven't used any of it myself. I suppose we'll all be using it soon! Did you hear—— Yes, Mrs. McLennigan 'phoned to me. She heard about it from Mrs. Larson. Isn't it *killing!* Go-o-od-by!"

Returning to the door, she took my letter and read it through.

"Oh!" she gurgled, leaning against the door casing, one hand pressed on her heart. "This is the funniest thing I ever heard of. Going into the movies! *Oh!"*

I told myself on the moment that women were queer in some ways. Certainly it didn't take much to amuse and interest them. Miss Prindle's letter wasn't funny to me.

I quit work at five o'clock, having sold nine boxes of soap. Tom was waiting for me at the corner of Church and Main. He had sold seven boxes. We hadn't gone very far before Scoop overtook us.

"I had quite a talk with Deacon Pillpopper," he told us. "He remembers the ten-ring puzzle. Says it's worth a lot of money and that we ought to try and find it."

"I didn't know," I said, "that puzzles were valuable."

"*He* seems to think," Scoop said, "that the Matson model could be sold to some toy company for several thousand dollars."

"Where do you suppose the puzzle went to?"

"It's probably hid with the money."

"Did you tell the deacon about the marked verses in the Bible?"

"Sure thing. He agrees with me that there is some connection between the ten-ring puzzle and the 'ten and ten' markings in the Bible. I'm to have another talk with him soon. And in the meantime he's going to drive out to Mrs. Kelly's house and see the Bible himself."

I fished Miss Prindle's letter out of my pocket, explaining to our leader how the letter had come into my possession.

"A trick of the Strickers," he said promptly.

"Nothing of the kind," I told him. "For I saw her myself. So did Tom."

"Rats! A woman can't become beautiful over night."

"Miss Prindle did," I waggled. "And so did Red."

"Red? Do you mean Red Meyers? Oh, ho, ho, ho! That's rich!"

"His mother used the beauty soap on him," I said, "and his freckles have all disappeared. His skin is like peaches and cream."

"I've got to see it," said Scoop, "to believe it."

So, to convince him, we went around by Red's house, learning from Mrs. Meyers that the beautiful one was sleeping.

"Has his freckles really disappeared?" Scoop quizzed.

"Ask Jerry and Tom," the woman smiled. "They saw him."

"Golly Ned!" cried Scoop, tugging at his hair. "I can't understand it. It doesn't seem possible to me. But it must be so if the three of you say so."

We started for the brick house.

"I wonder," grinned Tom, as we turned the corner, "if the soap will beautify all of our customers."

"Why shouldn't it?" I countered.

"If it does," he laughed, "this is going to be a badly mixed-up town. For half of the husbands won't be able to pick out their own wives."

It was indeed a laughable situation. We enjoyed talking about it. I guess, though, we would have been less hilarious if we had known the real cause of Miss Prindle's and Red's sudden beauty.

CHAPTER XIII

UP A ROPE

It was Scoop's scheme, as he now explained to us, to fly a kite to a purpose over the old mill. So, upon our arrival at the brick house, he and I went guardedly to an open spot on the windward side of the mill and from there released the kite into the air.

"Fine!" he chuckled, when the sagging string touched the mill roof.

I had told him that I would have no part in his proposed invasion of the enemy's territory. I had declared that it was entirely too risky for my blood. But what I had said had been largely a matter of talk. I'm no coward. I was ready, as his loyal chum, to stand by him.

As a matter of fact, in my courageous decision, I was even more impatient than he was for night to come. I'm that way by nature. Sometimes it takes me quite a while to make up my mind, but once I have decided to do a certain thing I like to go ahead and do it. I don't like to wait around.

And having completed our plans, I was impatient, as I say, for nightfall. For it was our intended scheme to climb a rope in the darkness to the mill's flat roof, gaining secret access at that unguarded quarter to the enemy's territory. The spy, of course, would be expecting us to come up the stairs—would probably have several hidden traps in readiness for us there. He never would think of the roof. That was the fun of it.

The kite properly raised, we had now to wait for the wind to go down, which it undoubtedly would do at sunset. And when Tom called us to supper, which he and Peg had prepared, we tied the kite string to a bush, hoping that in the time we were eating that the kite would "die," leaving its string on the mill roof. It was by the aid of this string, of course, that we expected to secretly raise our rope, pulling it up the east wall of the mill, over the top, then down the west wall, tying it to a tree.

Supper over, Tom and I called on the soap man, at Scoop's directions, not only to settle up with our employer and pay him the money due him, but to hold him in spirited conversation, in the mill, until our leader had returned from town with the necessary rope.

"If you hear me at work," Scoop had instructed, "sing a song or dance a jig. Do anything," he had added, with a grin, "that will make a lot of noise. I'll give two owl hoots when I'm through."

So we told the soap man funny stories, thereby keeping him in the mill until dusk. Shortly after eight o'clock a near-by owl went, "Hoo-o! Hoo-o!" At least the soap man thought it was an owl. We didn't tell him anything different. And in keeping with our leader's instructions, we yawned, telling the mill's tenant that it was time for us to go home.

"Everything's ready," Scoop told us, when we had joined him near the inventor's workshop.

"Rope up?" I inquired.

"Sure thing."

"We never heard you," said Tom.

"It was no trick to get it up. First, I pulled up a heavier cord, one that wouldn't be likely to break under the rope's weight, and then I pulled up the rope with the stronger cord."

We waited in the brick house until the clock struck nine. It was now dark enough for our purpose. There was some final conversation between the four of us. As on the preceding night, Scoop told Peg and Tom to be sure and keep the house doors locked, letting us in only on signal.

Then he and I set forth. Coming into the mill yard, we saw a light in the windows on the second floor. Thump! thump! thump! The spy was at work.

"I'll go up first," Scoop whispered, gripping the rope, which vanished into the overhead darkness. "Hold it tight, Jerry. When I get to the top I'll give it three quick jerks."

Two-three minutes passed. Then I got the signal. It was my turn now.

I had a queer feeling as I left the ground. It was as though I were climbing into space. What if the rope should break? I tried not to think about it, especially when I was ten or fifteen feet from the ground. It was a strong rope. Scoop had told me so. It had held him. I wasn't any heavier than he was. Certainly it ought to hold me.

But what if the spy, in suddenly detecting me, should reach out of a window and slash the rope with a knife? I shivered in the thought of it. Then I told myself that I was foolish to let such thoughts come into my head. I was in no danger from the spy. For I could hear his steady thump! thump! thump! With his stair traps, he felt quite secure, and wasn't giving any thought to what was going on outside of his windows.

I got out of breath after a minute or two. My arms began to ache. I wasn't used to doing this. Climbing a rope, let me tell you, is hard work. There is a trick to it, too. A lot of boys can't do it.

Twisting my feet into the rope to keep from slipping, I rested myself, then, after a few moments, continued my climb. I was even with the second-story windows now. It was on this floor that the spy was working. I could hear him, but I couldn't see him.

Scoop was waiting for me at the roof edge. He gave me a lift. I was glad, let me tell you, when I had something firm under my feet once again.

"Jinks!" I panted. "That was hard work."

"S-h-h-h! Get your wind, Jerry. Take your time. We've got all night."

I sat down on the roof, concluding that this was the quickest way to rest myself and get rid of the trembling in my arms.

As my wind came back, and the trembling diminished, I gave a curious eye to my surroundings. It didn't seem so dark now. I could trace the rectangle of the mill's roof. And I could distinguish the shape of near-by tree tops. In the direction of town I could see dozens of lights in houses and on street corners. This wasn't the first time that I had been on the mill roof—one time, in our play, the fellows had shut me up there for nearly an hour—but somehow the surroundings seemed strange and unfamiliar to me in the darkness. I had the feeling, too, that I was in danger of falling.

After a little bit I got up, ready for business.

A box-like shape stood out in the darkness ahead of us. This was the office that Mr. Matson had added to his mill. He had built it on the flat roof. There was no door opening onto the roof, but there were four windows, one on each side of the small building, and it was through one of these windows that we had planned to enter the mill.

But, to our disappointment, the windows were locked.

"Dog-gone!" muttered Scoop. "He's fastened them on the inside." There was a moment's silence. "Well," he added, "what are we going to do?"

"You're the leader," I reminded.

"That doesn't prevent you from speaking up if you get an idea."

My hand touched something on the roof building's outside wooden wall. I felt around for a moment or two.

"All right," I laughed. "I've got an idea."

"I'm listening."

"We'll go down the office chimney. Santa Claus stuff."

"Jinks!"

"Here's ladder steps," I told him, "leading to the roof. See? And you know how big the chimney is."

That was another queer thing that Mr. Matson had done: The fireplace that he had built in his crazy roof office had a chimney as big as a sugar barrel.

Having suggested the idea, I led the way.

"Get the rope," I whispered to Scoop from the small building's roof, "and come up and let me down the chimney."

With the rope tied under my arms, I got on the chimney edge and swung my legs into the black hole, sort of measuring the chimney with my feet. It was plenty big enough for me, I concluded, though it wasn't as roomy on the inside as I had thought it would be.

"As soon as I'm down," I told Scoop, "pull up

the rope and drop it to the ground where it was. For we may have to use it in a hurry. I'll let you in the east window."

"Check," said Scoop, meaning that he understood.

I had figured that the chimney, long unused and open to the weather, would be washed clean of soot. But that shows how little I knew about chimneys!

Soot! Man alive, in less than ten seconds I was plastered with it. I hardly dared to breathe. Blinded, my ears stuffed full of the nasty black stuff, I opened my mouth to tell Scoop to haul me up in a hurry. But I had so much soot in my mouth that I couldn't say a word.

Halfway down I got hooked on a nail that had been plastered into the bricks.

"Untie the rope," Scoop hissed down the black hole, thinking, of course, that I had landed at the bottom.

"Blub-blub-bub," I spit.

"What's that?" the rope handler hissed quickly.

"Blub-bub."

"What the dickens? . . . Are you trying to kiss yourself on the back of the neck?"

"I'b studk," I got out.

"Oh! . . ."

"Pud me ub," I gagged. "I'b fud ud sud."

He gave a quick jerk on the rope. Unhooked, I went kerplunk to the bottom of the chimney.

Sifting myself from the soot, sort of, I untied the rope and gave it a sharp jerk. Getting the signal, Scoop pulled the rope up the chimney. I heard him getting down from the roof. A few moments later he came to the east window, which I managed to get unfastened.

"Where are you?" he whispered.

"Here," I said, from in front of him.

"I can't see you."

Of course he couldn't see me! How could he, when I was seven shades blacker than the night, itself?

I told him what had happened to me. I told him how miserable I felt with the soot in my eyes and nose and mouth and ears. There was pecks of it down the back of my neck, I told him, and bushels of it clinging to my clothes.

He said he was sorry for me. But I could tell from the tone of his voice that he was giggling to himself. Well, to that point, I guess that *I* would have giggled if *he* had been the unlucky one to get into the soot.

Thump! thump! thump! The spy was at work

directly below us. There was need for caution. The wonder was that I hadn't been heard before this. For I hadn't landed quietly at the bottom of the chimney. Two skinned knees and a skinned nose gave testimony to that.

Moving stealthily to the door that opened onto the stairs, we squinted down. His candle stuck in an ink bottle, the old man was standing on a box tapping the stone wall with a hammer. In the flickering light he seemed to be more shabby and more hairy than ever. A wolf! That is what he was—a two-legged wolf. As we watched him, he tapped over a space two yards square. Marking the spot, he moved his box, beginning work on a new square. Plainly he was going over every inch of the mill wall in a systematic search for the puzzle maker's hidden fortune.

Did he have a clew to the money's hiding place? Did he know to a certainty that the money was cemented into the stone wall? I wondered to myself as I watched him.

If the money were in the wall, he would be sure to find it sooner or later. We had bragged to Mrs. Kelly and the granddaughter that we wouldn't let the uncle get away from us with the hidden fortune. But now I was suddenly uneasy in the thought that he might find the money ahead of us and escape us. It would be hard to keep track of him every minute.

" 'Ten and ten,' " Scoop whispered in my ear. "Do you see anything down there, Jerry, that looks like 'ten and ten'?"

"No," I breathed.

" 'Ten and ten.' Um. . . . Let me have your flashlight. I'm going to look around. Keep your eye on him, Jerry."

Ten-twenty-thirty minutes passed. I could hear Scoop tiptoeing around the office. But I didn't turn my head to see what he was doing. For the spy needed constant watching. Our goose would be cooked, as the saying is, if he came upstairs and surprised us.

Scoop touched me on the back.

"Jerry, do you notice anything peculiar about this room?"

"It has an awfully sooty chimney," I grumbled.

He chuckled.

"I wasn't thinking of the chimney."

"Huh!"

"The room is square."

"I knew that."

"Ten feet by ten feet."

"What?"

"I measured it. 'Ten and ten.' I bet anything

you want to bet that the money is hidden in this room."

"In the wall plaster?"

"Probably."

There was a sudden silence from below. Then we heard quick footsteps on the stairs.

"Out through the window, Jerry. *Quick!*"

We weren't a moment too soon.

"Let's go down the rope," I shivered, scared clear through.

"You go down. I'll follow in a few minutes. I want to peek through the windows."

Sliding to the ground, I waited there until my companion joined me.

"He came upstairs and went to bed," Scoop told me. "So I guess he won't need any more watching to-night."

"He'll get up at midnight," I said.

"What for?"

"He's been coming to the brick house every night at midnight."

"That's so. I wonder why he waits till midnight to try the doors. Queer."

"Everything he does is queer," I returned.

Scoop nodded.

"Gennor must have been hard up for a spy to hire *him*."

We went to the tree where the rope was tied.

"Do you really believe," I inquired, "that the money is hidden in the office?"

"I'd sooner think it's there than in the stone wall."

"The spy must have a clew though."

"He probably thinks he has. But it's plain that we've got a better clew than he has."

"How are we going to get the money?" I then inquired.

Scoop was pulling down the rope, coiling it on his left arm.

"What puzzles me more than that," he joked, laughing, "is how in Sam Hill we're going to get you cleaned up. You're a sight, Jerry. Just wait till Peg and Tom see you! They'll laugh themselves into a fit."

"But you haven't answered my question," I hung on.

"I can't tell you how we're going to get the hidden money," he said, "for, truthfully, I don't know. Come on. It's bedtime."

CHAPTER XIV

FELIX GENNOR, JR.

THE fellows had a lot of fun with me the following morning. Having given me a suit of his clothes to wear, my own being too filthy for further use, Tom hunted up an article in the back of Aunt Polly's cook book telling how to remove ink stains with sour cream. He said that if sour cream was good for ink stains it ought to be first-class for soot. So he and the others plastered sour cream all over my face. Then they rubbed me with coarse towels. But when they got through with me I was far from being white.

"It'll have to wear off," I said.

"Wait till your ma sees you," grinned Scoop.

"I can powder my face," I said, "and make it white."

"Hot dog!" cried Tom, and he ran into his aunt's bedroom and came back with her powder puff.

Peg was draped out of a front window.

"There goes the mail man," he cried, when I had finished powdering myself. "Maybe there's another letter from Aunt Polly. Come on, gang."

We went down the path lickety-cut. But there was no letter in the mail box. It was disappointing. For we had hoped for favorable news.

"Anyway," Peg broke the silence, "no news is good news. So let's look on the bright side. . . . What are we going to do this morning?—peddle soap?"

While we were talking, making our plans, sort of, an automobile came into sight from the country, a classy red roadster, driven by a boy our age. There was a screeching of brakes, and on the instant that the car came to a skidding standstill, Tom dove from sight into a lilac bush beside the path.

"It's young Gennor," he hissed at us from under cover. "Watch your steps, fellows! He's up to some trick in stopping here."

Maybe Scoop and I and Peg would have looked less dumb if we had been allowed a few seconds to sort of prepare ourselves to greet the enemy's chief with a graceful bow.

As it was, we stared open-mouthed. So it isn't at all surprising that the newcomer mistook us for boobs. We looked it, I imagine.

He had said something to us in stopping, but this had failed to register in our minds. And now he followed up, smart-like:

"What is this place, anyway?—a deaf and dumb asylum?"

Right off I got his measure. Smart aleck. All swelled up over his pa's money. Sort of fed fat on the idea that he could sit in his two-thousand-dollar roadster and bark orders at common, every-day kids and make them jump around and wait on him.

Well, I'm not much of a jumper when I meet a fellow like that!

"Did you say something?" I purred, sort of letting my neck out at him.

"I asked you," he said, "if the town up ahead is Tutter."

"Is it?" I inquired, turning to Scoop.

"It was," he nodded, "yesterday morning at this time."

"Tutter's the burg I'm looking for," informed smarty.

"When did you lose it?" I inquired, innocent-like.

"Lose it?"

"You said you were looking for it."

I was supposed to get wabbly knees under the

sharp scowl that he shot at me. But the old knee joints were out of wabbles this morning.

"Don't git fresh with me," he said darkly, "or I may taken a sudden notion to push your face clean through the back of your head."

"All in one push?" I inquired, steady-like.

His legs were out of sight in the car, so I didn't know what he measured standing up. But I figured that he wasn't much bigger than me. And what if he was? I wasn't scared of him.

"I guess," he said, important-like, "that you don't know who I am."

"Tell me," I returned, "and I'll fall over in surprise."

"My name's Felix Gennor, Jr. I suppose you've heard of the Gennor Radio Corporation."

"Yes, indeed," I said.

"Well, that's us," and he sort of pumped his chest full of air like a toad. He was good! "My father," he added, "owns the whole concern. Millionaire. Buys me everything I want. Gave me this little bus for a birthday present."

Little bus! I wondered what he called a Ford.

"And if you like the looks of Tutter," I said, trying to get a line on him, "is your father going to buy you that for your next birthday?"

"If the town looks good to me," he said, "and

my proposition is accepted, we may build one of our factories here."

"A radio factory?"

"Our new radio toy factory," he informed, with an important flourish of his hand.

I caught Scoop's signal to go cautious.

"What kind of radio toys are you going to make in this new factory?" I inquired.

"Talking toys, of course."

"Like . . . cats?"

"Certainly."

"And . . . chickens?"

He nodded.

"And . . . frogs?"

"Possibly."

"You're not sure about the frogs?"

"That's a detail to be taken up later. I'm like my father," and he swaggered his shoulders, sort of. "We don't bother with details. We hire men to do that."

My, but he was smart!

"I see," I nodded. "Maybe," I added, looking into his eyes, "you'll give *me* a detail job in this new factory that you're going to build."

He gave a mean laugh.

"Sure thing," he promised. "I'll put you to work winding up our electric fans."

I wanted to tell him that he'd likely find his "fan" wound up before I got through with him. But I kept shut on that.

"Evidently," I said, instead, "you're the general manager and the board of directors and the vice president of the company."

"Not—er—exactly. But I run things more or less. My father is teaching me the business. Told me I could skip school this month. He says I have a good solid head."

"He told the truth," I nodded.

It was good and solid, all right! Like a block of wood.

"My father went to New York yesterday morning. So I decided to come down here and close the—er—toy factory deal."

This free talk puzzled me. He seemed not to know who we were. Could this indeed be the case? And was it a happenstance, sort of, that he had stopped here at the Ricks' mail box, instead of a trick, as Tom had suspected?

I was not long left in doubt.

"Know a family around here by the name of Ricks?" smarty inquired.

Scoop on the moment draped himself over the mail box's lettered cover.

"Yes," he put in ahead of me, "we have a family in town by that name. A man, a woman and a boy. The man is an inventor."

"That's the fellow I want to see."

"Is he doing some inventing for you?" quizzed Scoop.

"Er—something on that order. What direction is his home from here?"

"Are you going to put up at the hotel while you're in Tutter?"

"Of course."

"Well, they'll tell you at the hotel where Mr. Ricks lives."

As the roadster disappeared into town, Tom tumbled out of the lilac bush.

"The big bluffer! Yes, he'll build a radio toy factory, all right, if he can steal Pa's talking frog."

Scoop followed the dust cloud with curling lips.

"Jerry," he said, "I've already made up my mind to get rich. For a fellow with money can have a lot of fun doing a lot of good. But if ever I act like that, I want you to take me out and pulverize me."

"The pleasure will be all mine," I grinned.

"Evidently," continued Scoop, bending his thoughts to the situation, "he hasn't talked with the spy or he should have known who we were.

And plainly he knows nothing definite about the talking frog. Jerry's questions brought that out. But he knows that Mr. Ricks is working on a radio toy. And if we're to believe him, he'll be around shortly to make some kind of a proposition."

"I don't trust him," Tom said darkly.

"Nor do I," Scoop said quickly. "But we'll listen. And maybe we'll find out what he means by all of this toy factory talk."

"I hope he starts something rough," I spoke up. "Sweet doctor! It'll be fun mixing up with *him.*"

Scoop caught my eye.

"Remember what I told you, Jerry? I said it wouldn't surprise me to have the enemy send another spy down here. I didn't miss it very far."

"We'll have two to watch now," I said, "instead of one."

On entering the kitchen a few minutes later we discovered that some one, in the time of our absence, had picked the lock on the cellar door.

Scoop's face was as white as a sheet as he dashed down the stairs.

"It's gone," he cried from the cellar. "The spy has been here and dug up the talking frog!"

CHAPTER XV

THE PRISONER

We felt pretty blue and sick-like over the theft of the talking frog. For now Tom and his pa and Aunt Polly would have to go to the poorhouse. The invention that was to have put them on Easy Street had fallen into the enemy's hands. It would earn a million dollars for the dishonest president of the Gennor Radio Corporation. But poor Mr. Ricks would get not one penny.

"I told you that young Gennor was tricky," cried Tom, as we stood beside the hole in the cellar's dirt floor. "Oh, why didn't we suspect that he had the spy in here digging up the frog!" and the speaker's arms went up in despair.

Scoop looked dizzy. But his thinker wasn't wholly stalled. And to tune it up he circled the cellar, tugging at his hair.

"We've got to act quick," he said to Tom, "if we hope to save your pa's invention." He turned to me. "Jerry, make a bee-line for the hotel and keep an eye on Gennor. If he leaves the hotel, get onto his trail."

"And what about you fellows?" I inquired.

"As I said a moment ago Gennor may not know that the spy has the talking frog. But he soon will know it unless we cut in. For the spy, knowing that the other is due to arrive in town, will go to the hotel to report. So keep your eyes peeled, Jerry, for the soap man. If he comes into the hotel with a package under his arm, grab it and run. We'll wait here to receive mister smarty in case he decides to pay us a visit. Under the circumstances I guess we won't be put into jail if we make him comfortable in one of the upper rooms and keep him there for a day or two."

My eyes were popping.

"You mean," I cried, excited, "that you're going to make him a prisoner?"

Scoop gave a queer, tight-lipped grin.

"Something on that order," he said, slowly wagging his head. "Only we won't call him a prisoner. He'll be our *guest*. See? And we'll be very attentive to him and feed him on the best there is in the house and read him to sleep if necessary."

I thought of the old man in the mill.

"Are you going to prison-up the spy, too?"

"Whatever is necessary," said Scoop, "to recover the talking frog."

"Maybe he's found the hidden fortune," I cried, "and is now making his get-away."

"You look after Gennor," Scoop told me, "and we'll look after the spy. Eh, Peg?"

"I'll keep an eye on mister spy," waggled Peg, his jaw squared.

"Hot dog!" I cried, jumping for the stairs. And I ran lickety-cut into town.

Coming within sight of the Commercial House, which is a rather small building and not big and showy like the towering city hotels, I slowed up. For I was puffing like a loose-jointed merry-go-round engine. Getting my wind, I walked naturally to the hotel door and squinted inside.

But contrary to what I had thought would be the case, Gennor wasn't in the hotel lobby. Nor was his car parked in front. I was scared for a moment in the thought that he had already met the spy and had left town with the stolen invention.

The hotel manager got his eyes on me and grinned.

"Howdy, Jerry," he said, good-natured-like.

If you can imagine a man so tall that he has to close up like a jackknife in order to get into a regular-size bed, that is Mr. Rufus Tomlinson, who shares the ownership of the Tutter hotel with his son, Mr. Charley Tomlinson. And he is about three points skinnier than an underweight toothpick. In our Halloween parades he usually takes the part of Uncle Sam. That is how he got his nickname.

Realizing that the sooner I located young Gennor the better for our purpose, I came quickly into the small lobby, squinting here and there.

"Where have you got him hid?" I inquired, as a starter.

"Heh?" said Uncle Sam, scrooching and craning his neck.

"I heard he was in town," I said. "So I came on the run to take a squint at him."

"Take a squint at who?"

"Felix Gennor, Jr.," I returned, "the wonderful boy millionaire from Chicago."

Uncle Sam's face went sort of screwed up.

"Um. . ." he mumbled, meditative-like. "Didn't know Mr. Gennor was a millionaire. Mebby I ought to 'a' put him in the bridal soot."

I pretended surprise.

"What," I cried, "you don't mean to tell me that you put him in an *ordinary* room? Now that's too bad. For he'll be offended, and we won't get the new toy factory."

"Toy factory?" scrooched Uncle Sam.

"I understand," I went on, "that he intends to build a radio toy factory here if he likes the town."

The other could hardly swallow this.

"Him? Pshaw! He's jest a boy."

"His father," I said, "is backing him in whatever he does."

A crafty light came into the narrowed eyes.

"Toy factory, heh? Um. . . ."

"It will be a big thing for the town," I waggled. "And those lots of yours down by the depot will be worth a thousand dollars apiece."

"I was jest thinkin' of them lots. . . . Has he got an option on a factory site?"

"Not yet," I said, "for he's just arrived."

"Of course; of course. Um. . . ."

"The thing for you to do," I said, "is to show him a lot of attention here in the hotel. Then he'll like Tutter and we'll get the toy factory. See?"

"I'll move his luggage into the bridal soot right away," nodded Uncle Sam, shuffling eager-like.

"How are you fixed for a bell-boy?" I inquired.

"Hain't got one at present."

"He suspects that this is a regular hotel," I said. "And whoever heard of a hotel without a bell-boy?"

"Mebby——"

"All right," I jumped in, "you've got me won over. So tote out the uniform and I'll flop into it."

The other looked sort of dizzy.

"Uniform?" he repeated. "Um. . . . I hain't got no sech thing."

"Then," I said, starting for the door, "the new bell-boy will have to furnish his own uniform."

I was filled with giggles as I ran down the street to our house. For I had a blinger of an idea. Finding the doors locked, I went in through a cellar window. And without a second's delay I beat it for the attic to get the messenger-boy suit.

I had worn this suit in a school play. It was made of bright red cloth, with brass buttons up and down the front of a monkey jacket, and gold braid on the seams of the long trousers. Also the peakless cap was decorated with braid and buttons.

I got dressed. And rubbing the powder from my face I grinned at the young darkey whose face was reflected in the bedroom mirror.

"Who are you?" I inquired.

"Ah's the new bell-boy," he replied, "an' mah name is Gawge."

"All right, George," I nodded, "let's see you grin."

"Ya', suh, boss; ya', suh."

"Fine!" I laughed; and rolling my other clothes into a bundle, I cut a bee-line for the hotel.

The lobby was full of excited men. For in the time of my absence Uncle Sam had 'phoned to the mayor and the president of the Chamber of Commerce and a lot more prominent business men. They were buzzing around young Gennor. And did he like it? I'll tell the world!

"Yes," he said, throaty-like, trying hard not to pull in his chest, "my father is the president of the Gennor Radio Corporation of Chicago. And we may build a factory here. It all depends."

"I'm sure," said the mayor, "that the town will meet you more than halfway."

"Yes, indeed," spoke up Mr. Fisher of the Chamber of Commerce. "If we could—ah—arrange to discuss the matter with your father——"

I knew why he paused. He couldn't quite convince himself that he would gain anything for the town by talking business with this boy. He was used to doing business with men.

But in the next ten minutes young Gennor's

swaggering lingo had them all guessing. About every other word was "I" this or "we" that. To hear him tell it, the world contained just three wonderful people: Felix Gennor, Sr., was one and Felix Gennor, Jr., was the other two.

And convinced that they had everything to gain and very little to lose, the business men got their heads together and cooked up a program to entertain the young visitor. They figured, I guess, that the more they did for him the better pleased his father would be. There was to be a get-together banquet in the hotel dining room; and one of the excited aldermen rounded up the band boys. Into the lobby they came, horns and bass drum and everything, and another such whanging and banging and tooting you never heard in all your life. I tell you it was exciting. Poor Mrs. Tomlinson came running from the kitchen, her glasses hanging on one ear, to see if the house was tumbling down. My cap got knocked off in the jam and bent out of shape under some one's foot. And the mayor cheered so loud that he shot his false teeth down the back of Mr. Fisher's neck.

Gennor was the only one who didn't enjoy the music. For he had to quit talking about himself and listen.

Well, in the course of an hour the band boys

sort of ran dry on tunes and the mayor and the others went home to get their speeches written down and memorized for the coming banquet, to which, of course, Felix Gennor, Sr., was to be invited, the guest of honor.

"Guess I'll go up to my room," Gennor said to Uncle Sam.

Here was my chance.

"Ya', suh, boss; ya', suh," I said, polite-like, popping into view. I bobbed my head and grinned, just as I had been taught to do in the school play. And if ever there was a surprised man, it was Uncle Sam Tomlinson!

Getting the key to the bridal suite, I started for the stairs, motioning to the other to follow me. Unlocking the door, I fussed around inside of the room just like a regular bell-boy, raising the windows and switching the lights on and off.

And what do you know if I didn't get a ten-cent tip!

"Thanks, boss," I grinned, bowing and scraping.

Gennor's eyes were narrowed suspiciously.

"Haven't I seen you before?" he inquired.

"Ya', suh, boss; ya', suh."

"Where?"

"Ya', suh, boss; ya', suh."

" MISTAH RICKS AM THE FUNNY GEN'MAN WHO MAKES MACHINERY THINGS ! "

Jerry Todd and the Talking Frog. *Page* 159

Scowling with disgust, he stripped off his coat. And having no further excuse to remain in the room, I reluctantly reached for the doorknob.

But the other stopped me.

"Just a minute," he said, running water into the lavatory basin.

"Ya', suh, boss; ya'——"

"Shut up! You've said that seventeen times in the last minute."

"Ya', suh——"

I dodged the bar of soap that he fired at me and grinned.

Drying his hands, he dropped into a seat at the writing desk and worded a short note, enclosing it in an addressed envelope.

"Know where that man lives?" he inquired, handing me the envelope.

"Ya', suh," I nodded, after a glance at the name. "Mistah Ricks am the funny gen'man who makes machinery things."

"That's him," said Gennor. "See that he gets this right away. And if you bring back an answer, I'll be likely to find another dime for you."

"Ya', suh——"

"Git!" he threatened.

I had no intention of leaving the hotel with

that note. For the spy might come while I was away. The thing to do, I concluded, was to find out what the note contained and 'phone to Scoop.

A few moments later I came quickly into the empty lobby and put in a call under Mr. Ricks' number.

"Hello," said Scoop.

"This is Jerry," I informed; and keeping my voice low, I quickly told the other what had happened.

"Read the note," he instructed, crisp-like.

I went through the note hurriedly, keeping my eyes on the door.

"Evidently," said Scoop, "he doesn't know that Mr. Ricks is out of town. And that bears me out in my theory that he hasn't talked with the spy. Have you seen anything of the soap man, Jerry?"

I told him that I hadn't.

"Peg went over to the mill about an hour ago. We haven't seen anything of him since."

There was some more talk. Scoop told me what to do. And in line with his instructions, I kept out of sight for ten-fifteen minutes. Then I went puffing to the door of the bridal suite.

"Well?" grunted young Gennor, when my knock had gained permission to enter.

"Mistah Ricks wasn't at home, suh. But you-all am to come to his house to talk business. The folks say so."

The listener scowled.

"What? *Me* chase after that hick inventor? I guess not! If he wants to get in on my proposition he's got to come here."

Something had to be done to make Gennor change his mind. And I jumped into a scheme of my own.

"Mah lan'," I said, rolling my eyes, "you-all should 'a' seen the funny talkin' frowg Mistah Ricks is gone an' 'vented. Ya', suh, boss."

A cunning look camped in Gennor's eyes.

"Did you see the talking frog?"

"Ya', suh," I replied truthfully.

"Um. . . . And you say Mr. Ricks wants me to come to his house?"

"The folks say they hain't a-goin' to sell the frowg to the other gen'man till they is talked with you-all, suh."

"What other man do you mean?"

"Aw calc'lates as heow he am a Milwaukee man, suh."

Gennor said something under his breath and grabbed his hat.

"What street do I take?" he inquired.

My directions put a sick look into his face.

"What?" he screeched. "You say that Mr. Ricks lives in the big brick house on the edge of town?"

"Ya', suh," I grinned.

And on the moment I wanted to let out a tickled whoop. For I knew well enough what was in his mind. But, of course, I kept shut.

"Git out of here," he said, savage-like, giving me a shove. And following me into the hall, he put the key of the locked room into his pocket and stomped down the stairs.

When he was well out of sight in the street, I 'phoned to Scoop. Then I went to the basement and skinned out of my fancy uniform, putting on the clothes that I had brought from home. Hiding the uniform behind a flour barrel, I whitened my face with the flour and crawled through a window into the alley.

Overtaking Gennor, I kept well behind. And when he turned in at the brick house and cranked the door-bell, I circled to the rear and tumbled in through the kitchen door.

The visitor was talking loudly in the front hall.

"Why didn't you tell me," he demanded, ugly-like, "that old Ricks lived here?"

"Is that a riddle," returned Scoop, "or a question?"

"Don't git fresh with me. . . . Where's the old man? I came to talk business."

"Oh! . . ." said Scoop. "Have a seat."

"I understand," said Gennor, after a moment, "that Ricks has perfected his talking frog."

"Well?"

"I'm here to buy it."

"Mr. Ricks may consider your offer."

Gennor raised in his seat.

"*May* consider it? Well, he better jump at it if he knows what's good for him."

"I'll tell him," said Scoop.

"Bring him here and I'll tell him myself."

"He isn't in the house just now."

There was a short silence.

"Say," scowled young Gennor, "if it's your game to hold me up, you're going to get left. See?"

"Mr. Ricks," said Scoop, "wants only what is coming to him."

"This invention of his belongs to our company, anyway."

"That's what *you* say."

"We hired him to do some work on a radio transmitter. And the talking toy idea came to him while he was on our pay-roll. My father says so. But we want to be fair. And we're willing to pay him ten thousand dollars for his invention."

"Ten thousand dollars," said Scoop, "wouldn't interest Mr. Ricks."

"And if we build our new toy factory here in Tutter," Gennor added, "we'll put him in charge of it."

"Did your father send you here to tell us that?"

"You ask him."

There was another silence.

"Suppose," suggested Scoop, "that we get down to brass tacks."

"Now you're talkin'," said Gennor.

"You say that you're ready to pay ten thousand dollars for Mr. Ricks' invention and put him in charge of a factory to be built in Tutter?"

"Yes," nodded Gennor, "if we build the factory here, he'll be appointed manager."

"But you aren't sure that the factory will be built here?"

"We're going into the radio toy game on a big scale. That was decided at the last directors' meeting. And it was further decided to locate old Ricks and make him an offer not to exceed ten thousand dollars. But we haven't decided where we'll build the new factory. It may be here. It may be in Chicago."

"I understand," said Scoop. "And does that complete your proposition?"

"I've got a paper——"

"Just keep it in your pocket. For we're signing no papers to-day."

"My! You talk as though you are somebody."

"I'm a friend of Tom Ricks'," returned Scoop, quiet-like, "if that means anything to you."

"It doesn't," and Gennor gave a mean laugh.

"Notwithstanding," said Scoop, in the same even tone, "it means something to Tom. For I've promised to stand by him and protect his father's invention."

"No one is trying to steal it."

"I'm not so sure about that."

"Say! Who do you mean?"

"I was looking at you."

"I'll push your face in."

"No danger of that," sneered Scoop. "You might *hire* somebody to do it for you, but you wouldn't dare to tackle the job yourself."

Gennor sprang to his feet.

"You're a big bluff," Scoop went on, in the same sneering tone of voice. "But you haven't fooled me in the least with this ten-thousand-dollar offer. For why should your father offer to *buy* the invention when he has hired spies to steal it?"

"I'll git you for this," screeched Gennor. And when Tom and I ran into the room, he sneered: "Three against one."

"Three against one," scowled Scoop, "is a fair game as compared to what your father is doing."

"He never intended to steal the invention."

"We happen to know better," said Scoop. "But don't pat yourself on the back when I tell you that the spies succeeded in getting the frog away from us. For your man will have no chance to turn it over to you; and that, of course, is what brought you to town."

Gennor's eyes held an expression of cunning satisfaction as he backed to the door. And wheeling suddenly he grabbed the knob.

"I locked the door," said Scoop, "when you came in."

The defeated one flew into a rage.

"This is a holdup! But you'll get no money from my father."

"We don't expect or want any of his money. But we do intend to keep you here till we recover the talking frog."

"You'll go to jail for this."

"So you say. . . . Git up those stairs."

"I won't."

But he did. For, bully that he was, he went scared to death when our leader started to roll up his shirt sleeves.

Scoop locked the bedroom door on the prisoner and put the key in his pocket.

"Better go outside, Tom," he advised, "and watch the windows. For we don't want him to wave a distress signal or otherwise attract attention."

CHAPTER XVI

CHASED BY A GHOST

FOLLOWING the enemy chief's imprisonment in Aunt Polly's spare bedchamber, I went to the old mill to tell Peg the exciting news and to find out from him how things were at his end.

We certainly had our hands full. Plainly, there would be no more soap peddling for the present. I was kind of disappointed in that, for we had earned several dollars as assistant beautifiers. And it is always pleasing to a boy to earn money.

I found my big chum on his stomach in the mill-yard weeds. The spy was in the mill he told me.

"You can hear him if you sharpen your ears. He's been thumping on the mill wall all morning."

"Queer," I reflected, "that he should steal the talking frog before he had located the hidden fortune."

"He probably had his orders to steal it today."

"Orders from young Gennor?"

"Of course."

"Then why doesn't he deliver the stolen frog at the hotel?"

"Give him time. The day's young."

I told the other about my bell-boy job.

"I bet it's fun," Peg grinned.

"I couldn't have worked it so slick," I said, "if I hadn't gotten mixed up in the soot."

On the way to the hotel I met the Stricker gang.

"How's Mr. Gallywiggle?" grinned Bid. "Is he still manufacturing beauty soap?"

"I hope so," I returned quickly, giving the questioner a cold eye. "For you certainly need a pile of it."

"Mr. Gallywiggle," he recited, flourishing his hands, "the man who has taken more warts from women's noses than all of the talking machines in the world. The man who——"

"How did you find out about it?" I cut in.

"Oh," he laughed, winking at his companions, "I met old fuzzy-wuzzy yesterday when I delivered Miss Prindle's beauty letter to him at the old mill."

My eyes went narrowed in sudden suspicion. Then, as quickly, I told myself that I was foolish to let myself be troubled by such thoughts. The

Strickers might have delivered the letter, but the letter itself was no trick of theirs. It couldn't be a trick, I concluded. For I had seen the transformed dressmaker with my own eyes.

"Did you know," grinned Bid, "that Douglas Fairbanks is in town?"

I kept shut. For I wasn't going to bite on his old gag, whatever it was.

"He's here to sign up Miss Prindle," the gang leader went on. "He wants her to be his leading lady. Five hundred thousand dollars a year. Better than pumping a sewing machine, hey? Oh, I tell you, your beauty soap is wonderful stuff."

"Beat it," I scowled. "You can't string me."

"You're awful smart, aren't you?"

"I'm not bragging about it."

The leader laughed and gave his companions another wink.

"We know something that you don't know."

"Haw! haw! haw!" went the gang. "Beauty soap. Haw! haw! haw!"

They didn't know much I told myself, turning stiffly away.

While I was on bell-boy duty that afternoon a factory site committee came to the hotel and waited restlessly in the lobby for more than an hour. But Gennor, of course, failed to keep his appointment. Finally they went away, muttering and wagging their heads.

Evening came.

"Whar's he gone to?" inquired Uncle Sam, sort of puzzled-like, when Gennor failed to appear on time at the supper table.

"Don't you know?" I countered, acting innocent.

This brought a scowl into the thin face.

"If I knowed," he snapped at me, "I wouldn't be askin', would I?"

It came eleven o'clock and the hotel was closed for the night. Thus released, I got into my everyday clothes and beat it for the brick house.

The shadows under the whispering pine trees seemed to crowd in on me as I ran up the path. My heart was in my mouth, sort of. I had the feeling that something was watching me—a hidden, formidable something. And on the instant all of the stories that I had heard about Mr. Matson's ghost jumped helter-skelter through my mind.

I was trembling when I came to the porch. I ran for the door. And finding it locked, I beat on the panels and cried to my companions to let me in.

Footsteps sounded on the hall floor.

"It's Jerry," I cried.

"Just a minute," said Scoop, fumbling with the key.

And now comes the part of my story that always gives Mother the shivers!

There was a sound from behind. And wheeling, I got the scare of my life. For coming at me out of the shadows was a white, vapory, gliding thing, shaped like a man, yet without arms or legs.

I screeched and pounded. And every second that Scoop fumbled with the lock the ghost glided closer and closer. Its invisible feet were now on the porch steps. I could detect a pair of horrible, consuming eyes.

"I've been using the wrong key," muttered the fumbler.

Well, I guess I would have jumped right through the door if it hadn't swung open.

I tumbled in a heap at my companion's feet. Sort of clutching his legs for protection.

"The ghost!" I screeched. "Shut it out—*quick!*"

CHAPTER XVII

THE CRAZY PUZZLE ROOM

In the excited moments that immediately followed my tumbling entrance into the brick house, I panted out a story of what I had seen.

Scoop shook his head.

"Your imagination, Jerry. For no one ever saw a *real* ghost."

I told him that it was no case of imagination.

"Then," he concluded, "it was some one playing ghost."

"But it had no arms or legs. And its eyes were hollow wells."

"A make-up," he waggled. Passing quickly to a window, he pressed his nose against the glass. "I can't see anything."

"Maybe," spoke up Tom, "it was the spy."

"If it was," Scoop said quickly, "Peg will know about it."

I looked around the room, missing my big chum for the first time.

"He's watching the mill," Scoop told me when I inquired where the missing one was.

By this time I was well over my scare. And I felt pretty foolish. For, as Scoop had said, there was no such thing as a real ghost. What I had seen was some one playing ghost.

But to what ends?

We put out the lights and peered through the windows. But the ghost had vanished. Nor could we in the moment detect a single suspicous outside sound.

I hadn't been in the house very long before Peg signaled on the window for us to let him in.

"Where were you," I asked quickly, "when the spy chased me?"

He stared at me.

"Chased you? What do you mean?"

I told him about the ghost.

"It wasn't the spy," he waggled. "For the old man hasn't been out of the mill for hours. It was only within the past ten minutes that he quit his wall pounding and went to bed."

"The dickens!" cried Scoop, bewildered. "If it wasn't the spy, who was it?"

"Maybe," suggested Tom, "it was a second spy, one that we haven't seen."

"An unknown spy!" cried Scoop. There was

a short silence. "You may be right. But what's his object in playing ghost?"

It was indeed a mystery. In our conversation we advanced various scattered theories. The unknown spy, working alone, didn't know that the talking frog had been stolen; he was trying to frighten us away in order to gain possession of the invention; or, if he knew that the frog had been stolen by his companion spy, he was working to gain the release of his chief, our upstairs prisoner. Such, in substance, were our theories. But how widely we missed the mark was proved by later events.

On Sunday, the following day, we took turns guarding the old mill. For we were determined that the spy shouldn't escape from us with the recovered fortune if it were in our power to prevent it. Then, too, we talked of ways of getting into the mill, without the soap man's knowledge, to hunt for the stolen invention. We were quite sure that the talking frog was there.

We still had the rope that Scoop and I had used the night that we got into the mill by way of the roof. But we didn't dare to use it. It was hardly to be doubted that the soap man had discovered the unlocked window and the pile of soot in the fireplace. We may have left further evidence of our visit. And, in watching for us, he might cut our rope.

Our prisoner gave us no trouble. He seemed to take his confinement as a lark. We would gain nothing by holding him, he said. We would have to turn him loose sooner or later. So why should he worry? He was being well treated and was getting three square meals a day.

Then Monday morning came. We had given no thought to school. And when the first bell rang, we stared at one another blankly.

"What are we going to do with Gennor?" puzzled Scoop. "We dassn't skip school and stand guard here; and if we leave him alone he'll surely escape."

"I wouldn't want to go to school," I spoke up, "and leave him here by himself. Suppose the house should burn down! If anything were to happen to him, it would go hard with us."

Scoop grimaced and shrugged his shoulders.

"I guess," he concluded, "that the only thing for us to do is to turn him loose, as he has been expecting us to do. Blame it! Our luck's against us."

"It was a foolish trick," Peg criticized, "to imprison him in the first place. For we haven't gained anything."

"We've kept him from getting his hands on the talking frog."

"Yes, but *we* haven't got the frog. We're right where we were last Saturday."

"We know where the frog is."

"We think the mill spy has it. But we aren't sure."

"I've tried to pump Gennor," Scoop said, "but I didn't get anywhere. He's shrewd. When I asked him how many spies his father had hired, he laughed at me."

Our prisoner, naturally, was very much elated over our decision to turn him loose. But in leading up to the proposed release, our leader, to protect us, made the enemy promise to leave town.

"Which is a thing you'll want to do anyway," Scoop said. "For the Tutter business men will make it pretty hot for you when they learn how you fooled them."

"Who said I fooled them?" bluffed Gennor.

"You made them think that you were going to build a toy factory here."

"Maybe we will."

"That's hot air and you know it."

Gennor broke his promise about leaving town. And when we met him in the street that noon he gave us the horselaugh.

I'll hand it to him for having nerve. For what do you know if he hadn't taken out a ten-day option on a factory site! As a result, everybody in town was talking excitedly about the proposed new toy factory. And no one talked any louder or longer than Gennor himself.

"He must have the talking frog," I said, gloomy-like. "Otherwise he wouldn't be so sure of himself."

"Yes," said Tom, his face white, "we're licked."

"Not yet," waggled Scoop. "We've got a chance of winning out if your pa and Aunt Polly get to Washington first."

This thought brought some small satisfaction. But our spirits went baggy at the knees when a telegram came while we were eating dinner.

The inventor, Aunt Polly wired, had not been located. And the little old lady was now searching for him in Charleston, South Carolina.

Peg had been over to the old mill.

"The spy's still on the job," he told us, coming into the house when we were washing the dinner dishes.

His mention of the spy filled me with sudden anger.

"Why don't we get him out of there?" I cried.

"We'll monkey around until he finds the money and beats it."

The front door bell rang.

"It's Mrs. Kelly," Scoop told us, squinting under the door curtain.

The woman had a worried look as she came into the house.

"Sure, I thought I'd stop in an' find out what you boys have been doin'. For several days have passed an' I haven't heard a word from you. It's sick I am with worry in the fear that the rascally twin brother will git away from here with the money."

"He's still searching for it," Scoop told the visitor, "but, lucky for us, he isn't doing his searching in the right place."

"No?"

"We know where the money is, Mrs. Kelly."

"You do?"

"Have you ever been in the old mill?"

"Many times."

"Then you should know about the office."

"Office?"

"The small building on the roof."

"You mean the crazy puzzle room."

"What's that?" cried Scoop, straightening.

"Sure, the buildin' that you just mentioned was put up when Mrs. Matson was alive. She wouldn't let the ould gintleman mess around the house with his puzzles, so he built himself a room on the roof of his mill where he could work undisturbed. And because his wife said that he was fiddlin' away his time like a crazy man, the new workshop was called the crazy puzzle room."

"I was told," said Scoop, "that it was an office."

"Sure, the ould gintleman would have been crazy, indeed, to have built an office on the roof of his mill! No, the buildin' never was intended for an office, though a lot of people got that idea. It was, as I have just told you, a workroom."

"We think the money is hid in the room's plastered walls," said Scoop.

"An' what gives you that idea?"

"Because the room is ten feet square."

Mrs. Kelly knitted her forehead.

"'*Under* ten an' ten,'" she muttered, thinking. Her eyes lighted up. "Sure, the money is under the floor, boys, not in the wall."

"Under the floor?" cried Scoop.

"Deacon Pillpopper came out to call on me the other day to see if *he* could solve the Bible's secret; and as soon as he set eyes on the marked verses he said their meanin' was '*under* ten an' ten,' and not just 'ten an' ten.' "

" '*Under* ten and ten,' " repeated Scoop, his eyes dancing. "You're right, Mrs. Kelly. The penciled marks were *under* the chapter headings and verses. '*Under* ten and ten.' Hot dog! We can find the money in a jiffy."

"But how are we going to get the spy out of the mill?" I spoke up.

Laughing, Scoop told us his plan.

"I shall be on needles an' pins," worried Mrs. Kelly, "until I learn how you come out. Be careful, boys. Don't let the ould scoundrel come in an' surprise you."

When the visitor had gone, we got together a collection of axes, crowbars and hammers. We would need these tools when the time came to tear up the office floor.

"Now," grinned Scoop, "we'll go to school by way of the old mill and have a chat with soapy. He'll be tickled, I imagine, to learn that we're going to do some more soap peddling for him."

CHAPTER XVIII

THE TEN-RING PUZZLE

As on another day, we found the mill's tenant cooking his food over the smoky oil stove.

"What?" he scowled, pretending surprise at sight of us. "Be you boys alive yet? I figured you was all dead an' buried."

We knew what he meant. He was grouchy because we hadn't been working for him lately.

"We're in school now," Scoop said. "But we'll work for you to-night after four o'clock if you want us to."

"Um. . . After four o'clock, hey? I'll be lookin' fur you."

"We've covered the whole town," our leader followed up, "so we'll have to work in the country."

"You kin work anywhere in the county fur all of me."

Scoop scratched his head.

"A thing I hate about the country," he said,

"is the distance between the farmhouses. It takes so long to get from one house to another that a fellow can't do enough business to make it pay."

"You ought to have bicycles," the old man said.

"What we need," Scoop said, "is a horse and buggy."

The faded eyes were greedy in their expression.

"Mebby I kin let you borry Romeo."

"I hate to drive other people's horses," hesitated Scoop. "For I'm not a first-class driver." Then he brightened. "I've got it!"

"Um. . ."

"You can do the driving and we will do the peddling."

"Um. . ."

"We ought to sell at least ten dollars' worth," Scoop ran on, sort of letting the "ten dollars" rumble around under his tongue. It made it sound bigger. "And to pay you for driving us around in your buggy, we'll take only ten cents out of every quarter."

"Um. . ."

"We'll be here a few minutes after four. So be sure and have Romeo hitched up. For we don't want to waste any time."

It was our leader's scheme for two of us to go

with the soap man while the other pair tore up the puzzle room floor. It would be exciting to find the murdered man's hidden fortune. And, of course, we all wanted to stay in town. So, to be fair, we drew cuts. In this way it was decided that Tom and I were to go into the country while Scoop and Peg went to the mill. I was disappointed, but I didn't say anything. For a fellow can't expect to have things his own way all the time.

But I soon lost my depression. For on the way to school I got a sudden idea. I told the other fellows about it. If we could work it, it was very probable that Tom and I could get back to town in time to help with the treasure hunting, leaving the soap man in the country.

By running, I had time, before the last bell rang, to go to Dad's brickyard office. He wasn't there. But I told his stenographer to ask him for me to take my bicycle along with him in the auto when he drove to the east clay pit that afternoon, leaving the wheel at the Crandon farm. I was intending to go to the Crandon farm in a buggy, I explained to Miss Tubbs, and wanted the bicycle to ride home on. She promised to deliver my message. I have a fine pa. We do things for each other. I knew I could depend on him.

When I was passing into the school room that noon, Bid Stricker stopped me.

"Did you know," he grinned, "that William S. Hart is trying to get Miss Prindle to break her contract with Douglas Fairbanks and sign up with him?"

"Chase yourself," I scowled.

"Honest. He was in town this morning."

"And *I* heard," Jimmy Stricker spoke up, poking his nose into the conversation, "that Tom Mix is due in town to-morrow."

Bid sort of rolled his eyes at the ceiling.

"Isn't it wonderful," he sighed, "what a little soap will do?"

Why did they keep talking about the beauty soap and about Miss Prindle going into the movies? I wondered.

When Tom and I arrived at the mill at the conclusion of the day's school, the soap man had Romeo hitched to the buggy. We got in, one on each side of the driver, with the satchel of soap at our feet.

"Git up," the old man clucked, flapping the lines, and in response Romeo sort of collected his wabbly joints and leaned forward until he was in motion.

"We'll go over in the Crandon neighborhood,"

I spoke up. "Follow this road to the first turn, then go to the right."

It was four-thirty when we came within sight of the Crandon farm. Taking six cakes of beauty soap in my hands, I scrambled out of the buggy in front of the farmhouse, motioning to Tom to follow me.

"You wait here in the road," I told the soap man.

When Mrs. Crandon, a cousin of Dad's, opened the door, Tom and I stepped quickly into the farmhouse kitchen. I had been here a number of times to Sunday dinners. Chicken and hot biscuits and gravy. Um-yum! The thought of it made me hungry.

"I've been expecting you, Jerry. Your wheel's here."

"I know it."

"How did you come out?" she smiled, curious.

I told her about the old soap man. He was trying to steal some money, I said, that belonged to some one else, and we were trying to save the money for its rightful owner.

"Gracious me!" she cried, in sudden alarm.

"Tom and I are going back to town on my bike," I explained, "and we want you to keep the old soap man out in front as long as you can. When he tumbles to the fact that we have disappeared, you mustn't tell him where we have gone to."

"I won't," she promised.

"Here's some soap," I grinned, giving her my six cakes. "In a few minutes go out to the buggy and say: 'I believe I'll take another six cakes.' The old man will think that we're in here. And he'll be tickled pink to let you have all of the soap that you want. Then you can wait another two or three minutes and go out and get some more soap. See?"

Mrs. Crandon gave a hearty laugh.

"What if he tries to make me pay for the soap?"

"Tell him that you've changed your mind about buying it, and hand it back to him."

My bicycle, she told us, was in the carriage shed. Getting the wheel, we cut through an orchard to the country road. With Tom on the cross-bar, I pedaled for dear life.

We got to town before five o'clock. The brick house was closed. So we knew that our chums were still in the mill.

"Dog-gone!" cried Scoop, sweating, when we

came to the room where he and Peg were at work. "We've ripped up the whole floor and haven't found a thing."

Peg was smashing the brick hearth of the fireplace.

"Get busy, fellows," he panted. "We haven't a minute to spare."

Tom and I gave a cheerful hand to the work. Suddenly the awfulest groan fell on our ears that you can imagine. A sort of shivering, rattling groan.

"The miser's ghost!" I screeched, dropping my pick. "It's coming up the stairs!"

There was a rippling laugh from below. And who should come into sight but the grinning Matson girl.

"Don't ever tell me," she laughed, "how brave boys are. For I certainly had the four of you scared to death."

Scoop scowled.

"What's the idea?" he growled.

"Oh, I just did it for fun."

"Huh!"

"I wanted to be here to help you. So I coaxed Mrs. Kelly to bring me to town. She's at the house."

"You haven't helped us any by scaring us,"

grunted Scoop. Then he sort of cooled off and told the newcomer, in better manners, where the soap man was.

"We've got to hurry," he concluded, "if we expect to find the hidden fortune before the spy gets back to town."

"Let me help you," the girl offered quickly.

"It will be a big help to us," Scoop told her, "if you'll go below and watch for the enemy. If he comes before we're through up here, yell 'jiggers.' "

Well, we kept on smashing the bricks. And pretty soon we disclosed a metal box.

"The money!" I cried, excited.

The box was about a foot long by four inches wide and three inches deep. Its padlock was so rusted that we knew no key would ever unlock it. The only way to get the box open would be to break the padlock with a hammer.

Scoop shook the box, rattling its contents.

"Gold!" I cried.

"Shall we break it open, or shall we let the girl open it? It's hers."

"We better hand it over to her as it is," advised Peg.

We started for the stairs, anxious to get away from the dangerous territory.

"I guess old soapy will get an awful shock when he comes home and sees how we've messed up his sun parlor," laughed Scoop, looking back at the torn-up floor.

"He'll want to kill us," I shivered.

"He ought to be in jail," grunted Peg.

"I'd feel a lot safer," I said quickly, "if he *was* in jail."

A horse whinnied.

"Romeo!" cried Scoop, stopping abruptly on the stairs.

" 'Jiggers,' " a voice called.

Peg saw my white face.

"Don't be scared, Jerry. He can't get us. When he comes into the mill, we'll go down the rope. We've got it ready."

So down the rope we went, joining the girl in the mill yard.

"Here's your grandfather's fortune," Scoop grinned, handing her the metal box.

She gave a cry. It was the gladdest, happiest cry I had ever heard. And she took the box and hugged it in her arms.

"Oh!" she cried.

We could hear the soap man in the mill.

"Let's go over to the house," suggested Scoop, "where we can lock ourselves in if necessary.

For we don't know what the old coot is liable to do."

Fortified in the brick house, we broke open the metal box. But, to our disappointment, it contained no money. Not a penny. Its only content was the ten-ring puzzle that Mr. Matson had made just before he met with his awful death.

"There's money hid somewhere," cried Mrs. Kelly. "I know it. For the ould gintleman told me so."

"He might not have been telling you the truth."

"He was rich. If the money isn't hid, where is it?"

"Maybe," spoke up Peg, "it's cemented into the mill wall, as the spy seems to think."

Mrs. Kelly got ready to leave for home.

"To-morrow," she said, sort of decisive-like, "I'm goin' to see the judge an' tell him the whole story. He'll know what to do."

CHAPTER XIX

SCOOP DISAPPEARS

CONTRARY to what we thought would be the case, the soap man didn't come near us. And shortly after six o'clock we saw him leave the mill yard in his rickety buggy, heading south. When he had disappeared from our sight we drew a deep breath. It was our hope, of course, that we had seen the last of him.

But we hadn't, as you will learn by reading on.

In a way we had made a mess of things. We had let the enemy get the talking frog away from us; and we had fumbled in recovering the murdered puzzle maker's hidden fortune. Of course, if we were to believe Deacon Pillpopper, the ten-ring puzzle had a certain money value. But it wasn't what we had expected to find. Far from it. Moreover, the puzzle was useless to us without the directions for working it. We couldn't do a thing with it.

In going to bed that night we agreed that there

was no need to stand guard. For most certainly we had seen the last of the enemy's spies. And that meant that we had seen the last of the ghost.

I was tired and went promptly to sleep. It seemed to me that not more than ten minutes had elapsed when a whispering voice told me to get up. The clock on the lower floor struck midnight.

"There's some one at the kitchen door," Scoop told me.

Having been awakened ahead of me, Peg and Tom were standing in a puddle of moonlight that came through the bedroom window. Half asleep and half awake I got onto my feet.

"I went to the kitchen to get a drink," Scoop told us. "I didn't bother to light a lamp. I heard footfalls on the porch. Then the doorknob turned."

We went noiselessly down the stairs, more bewildered than frightened. And sure enough, as Scoop had said, some one was trying to push our key out of the lock of the kitchen door.

I crept to a near-by window, detecting the ghost on the porch. A startled cry sprang to my lips. And thus warned of our presence in the kitchen, the prowler glided swiftly from the porch into the shadows.

Scoop ran into the sitting room and threw up a window.

"I'm going to find out who it is," he said, grim-like. "Wait here at the window. For you might have to drag me in quick."

Then he went out through the opening. I leaned over the sill and watched him creep to a corner of the house. The kitchen porch was now within range of his eyes. Suddenly he vanished.

The minutes dragged along. I took to counting the pumping strokes of my heart. Thump! thump! thump! Once Tom sneezed. I almost jumped out of my skin.

My legs went stiff and cramped from crouching in one position. Why didn't Scoop come back? I hung over the sill to catch possible sight of my daring chum. But nowhere was he within range of my anxious eyes.

"He's been gone an hour," Tom said in a queer, hushed whisper.

It came two o'clock; three o'clock; four o'clock. And still Scoop hadn't returned.

At daybreak we went outside and circled the house. I was sick with worry. For I realized that something had happened to my chum. Maybe he had been murdered. And the ghost was the murderer.

But who was the ghost? I thought of the old soap man. Was *he* the ghost after all? It wasn't impossible.

Somehow, though, I had the feeling that the soap man wasn't the ghost. And in trying to probe the confusing mystery I acknowledged bewilderment.

Then we found this message chalked on the mail box:

Lay low till I get back.
SCOOP.

I went suddenly happy. For Scoop was alive. He was up to some scheme. He had a reason for vanishing.

Thinking that he might show up in time for breakfast, we set a plate for him. But only the three of us shared the meal. Then we went to school. The teacher wanted to know where Howard Ellery was. But no one could tell her.

It came noon. And Scoop hadn't returned.

Stopping in at the hotel on the way to school, I found Uncle Sam Tomlinson fretting over the absence of his star guest.

"Has he gone back to Chicago?" I inquired.

"How do I know whar he's gone to?" the

other scowled. "He was here at ten o'clock last night. But he hain't been seen since. An' my wife says as how his bed is jest the way she made it up yesterday."

I ran to the near-by garage. Gennor's red roadster was in storage. This proved that its owner hadn't left town.

But where was he? And, more important in my mind, where was Scoop?

The school bell summoned the three of us to our books. But the pages might just as well have been printed in Chinese for all of the understanding that we got out of them that afternoon.

Our thoughts were of Scoop. He was in danger. And we wanted to be with him so that we could help him. Not knowing where he was, or what was happening to him, made us crazy, sort of.

CHAPTER XX

UP THE RIVER

AFTER what seemed an age to us, it came time for school to be dismissed for the day. And with anxious hearts Tom and I and Peg hurried home. We were hopeful that Scoop would be waiting for us at the brick house. And in this we were not disappointed.

He was seated cross-legged at the kitchen table making ham sandwiches and swigging down milk.

"This," he told us, with a weary grin, "is my breakfast, dinner and supper."

Our tongues waggled with eager questions bearing on his adventure. But he shook his head, motioning to us to be patient until he was through eating.

I could see that he was doing some hard thinking as he got on the outside of his food. Finally he pushed back from the table and loosened his belt.

"Well," he said, giving us a queer look, "I think I know who's got the talking frog."

I immediately guessed young Gennor, explaining to our returned leader about the Chicago kid's sudden disappearance.

Scoop waggled with understanding.

"I know all about that," he said. "For last night I followed Gennor to the old Windmere Hotel. He was there until an hour ago."

"*In* the hotel?" I inquired, staring in unbelief.

"Watching it," Scoop said, "from the outside. And I, in turn, have been watching him. When he came to town, I followed."

"But why should he go to the old hotel? It's been closed for years."

"Because," returned Scoop in a steady voice, "he suspects that the talking frog is there. I want to tell you that kid is no dummy! Hearing us tell about the ghost put him hep to things that *we* never dreamed of. And he came here last night to learn who the ghost was. For it was his hunch—and he had the right dope—that the ghost was the frog thief."

"And didn't he know that the ghost was one of his father's spies?"

"*He* knew," Scoop said steadily, "that the

ghost *wasn't* a spy. That's where he had the advantage over us."

"And it was the ghost who dug up the talking frog and not the spy?"

The other nodded.

"But who is the ghost?"

I was tingling with excitement. For I could tell from Scoop's mysterious actions that he was holding something back.

"That," he returned, "is what you and I are going to find out."

"And you don't know?" I cried, trying to pin him down.

"I suspect who it is," he said. "But if I were to tell you, you'd say that I was crazy."

And that is exactly what I did say when my coaxing had brought out the name.

"But even if you are right," I said, coming from under my dazed amazement, "why should *he* steal the talking frog?"

"I can't answer that, Jerry. I only know that he was here last night. Your cry scared him away. Gennor and I followed him to the old hotel—though the other kid, of course, didn't know that I was trailing along behind."

"And you say the ghost is living in the old hotel?"

"Apparently."

"But if the talking frog is there," I followed up, giving him a puzzled look, "why didn't you go in and get it?"

"Jerry, tell me the truth. Under the circumstances would *you* have gone alone into that old deserted building?"

I quickly admitted that I wouldn't have had the courage. For the risk was plain.

"I could tell from Gennor's actions," Scoop went on, "that *he* wanted to go in where the ghost was, but, like myself, he didn't dare to. What kept him there all day was the hope that the ghost would leave. Nothing doing. . . . I have a hunch that he's in town to get the Strickers to help him. I've seen Bid riding around in the red car. We've got to shake a leg. For the whole gang may be speeding for the river this very minute in the enemy's auto. You can see what we're up against."

Yes, it was a time for quick action. We had to get to the old hotel ahead of the others. And it was decided on the moment that Scoop and I should make the trip. Tom and Peg were to lay low in the brick house.

"And when the ghost comes to-night," instructed Scoop, "don't scare him away. Let him have free run of the house. But watch what he does. He has a reason in repeatedly coming here. And only in learning what his reason is will we be likely to solve the mystery. I'm hoping that Jerry and I will be back in time for the big show."

It was somewhat after five o'clock when Scoop and I left the brick house. Hurrying through town, we came to the long bridge spanning the Illinois River. The Windmere Hotel road was on the opposite side of the river. But instead of entering the bridge, as I had expected him to do, the leader turned to the right, entering Deacon Pillpopper's yard and knocking on the kitchen door.

"Well, well," cackled the old boat renter, tickled-like, "if it hain't Scoop an' Jerry! Come right in; come right in," he invited politely. "I was jest gittin' ready to set up an' eat. Hain't got a turrible sight cooked, but you're welcome to share what I've got. Jest shove that ol' cat off its box, Jerry, an' draw up to the table."

Scoop shook his head, explaining that we were in a hurry.

"We're headed for the old Windmere Hotel," he said, "and we've got to get there quick. For a stolen invention has been hid there, and a friend of ours is liable to suffer if we delay a minute in recovering it. We can get there quicker in a motor-boat. And under the circumstances I'm going to ask you to let us borrow your small launch. We haven't any money to pay you, but if things work out as I hope, you'll get enough pay to buy a brand new launch and a rowboat or two thrown in. Can we take it?"

"Well, neow," the old man waggled, "I'd say 'no' right off to most b'ys. But I hain't afeered to trust you. I know you'll be keerful. Besides, I hain't furgot 'bout that bag of apples you brought me last fall."

Full of gratitude for his kindness, we ran to the river pier. I untied the boat while Scoop turned on the gas and electricity. Having been out in the boat with its owner, we knew how to run it.

"Here we go!" cried Scoop, getting ready to press the control lever into "forward."

I yelled to him to hold up.

"The deacon's coming on the run. Maybe he wants to go along."

But that wasn't the case.

"The ten-ring puzzle," the old man wheezed. "Have you found it, b'ys?"

We told him that we had.

"I knowed it was the puzzle that the Bible markings had reference to. Miz Kelly said it was money that was hid. I said, 'No, it hain't money, it's the ten-ring puzzle, which is jest as good as money, though. You kin sell it any day in the week,' I told her, 'fur a thousand dollars or better.' "

"We've got it," grinned Scoop, "but we don't know how to work it."

"Um. . . Let *me* git a whack at it."

"We'll bring it over to-morrow."

"You didn't find any money 'long with the puzzle?"

"Not a penny."

The old man scratched his head.

"They may be money hid, all right. Fur, as Miz Kelly says, the old man was rich. . . . I'm goin' to have another look at that Bible."

Headed up the river, we presently came to the new Woodlawn Bay Hotel, which is the up-to-date resort that put the old Windmere House out of business. For summer guests preferred the new hotel. Unable to make it pay, the old hotel closed up. That was six-seven years ago.

Another mile and we came to the rotting pier of the shut-up Windmere House. Here things looked deserted and gloomy. The barn-like building stared back at us with its three tiers of window eyes. I dreaded to enter. And speculating in my mind on its hidden dangers, I went sort of shivery in the knees.

We tied the launch to the pier.

"See anything of Gennor and his gang?" inquired Scoop, squinting ashore.

"Maybe they're in the hotel."

"We'll circle the building and see if the red car is here."

But to our satisfaction the roadster was nowhere in sight in the hotel yard.

"Come on," motioned Scoop, starting for a rear door.

I didn't hurry.

"Do you suppose," I said, sort of letting out my neck in all directions at once, "that the ghost is watching us through one of those windows?"

"He probably is," returned Scoop, "if he's inside. For I happen to know that he isn't blind. And he must have heard our motor."

I began to sweat.

"It's awful risky," I said, "going in there."

"Tell me something that I don't know."

"I hate to see you do it," I went on. "For he might kill you. And being my best pal, I've got to look out for you."

"You needn't worry about *me,*" grunted Scoop. "I know how to take care of myself."

"But what are you going to do if he jumps at you?"

"Fight, of course."

"If he jumps at *me,*" I said truthfully, "I'll drop dead."

"You're trying awful hard," Scoop grinned, "to make me think that you haven't any grit. But I know *you,* ol' timer! Come on."

The door was unlocked. And stepping into the musty, dirty kitchen, I expected nothing else than to get a whang on the head.

Scoop dropped to his hands and knees, examining the footprints in the floor's coating of dust.

"A man's," he waggled, "and all of a size. So we know the Strickers haven't been here. Buck up, Jerry. I have the feeling that we're going to walk out of here with the talking frog."

"And I have the feeling," I groaned, "that we'll be carried out in pieces."

"The tracks go this way," Scoop said, advancing.

"I wish my tracks were going the other way."

"Let's not talk," he advised. "The ghost might hear us."

"I hope he does," I said, "and runs."

This kind of crazy talk sort of stiffened my wabbly knees. And soon I was keeping abreast of my companion, just as brave as he was.

We followed the tracks up two flights of stairs to the third floor, then down a long hall. The closed chamber doors on our right and left gave me an uneasy feeling.

We were now almost to the hall's end. Pausing, we sharpened our ears. Then we crept to a closed door where the tracks showed in and out.

"Hands up!" he shouted, pushing open the door and bounding into the room.

But the ghost wasn't there!

Another such room I never expect to see. Here and there were odds and ends of discarded furniture. Two rickety chairs, a cluttered bureau, a three-legged table. An old oil stove had smoked black the wall behind it and the ceiling directly overhead. The dirty cupboard was filled with greasy pots and pans. It was hard to conceive how a man could live in such stinking filth.

A bed was set up in an adjoining room, reached through a connecting door. Here windows on two sides looked down upon the river and a clutter of rotting sheds. Also we could trace the course of the weedy, incoming road.

Opening a closet door, Scoop pointed to a man's tattered raincoat. There was a worn pair of shoes on the floor. We pawed through a litter of paper and other trash, but failed to uncover the talking frog.

At this point the pur of a motor fell on our ears. Then we heard boys' voices. Gennor and his gang had arrived. We realized that it was them, even before we had gotten sight of them from the chamber window.

Bid got his eyes on our motor-boat.

"Lookit!" he screeched, pointing. The whole gang ran to the river's edge. We were afraid that they would untie the boat or damage the engine.

Gennor came running from his car with an old leather traveling bag of peculiar shape. Lining up the others in a bossy way, he advanced on the hotel.

Hearing them on the stairs, and realizing that we were trapped, sort of, Scoop shot the bolt in the connecting door. This gave us the bedroom as a fortress.

The others tumbled into the adjoining room.

"What do you know about this?" cried Bid. "Somebody's living here."

"Let's have some refreshments," laughed Jimmy, and we could hear him rustling paper bags. "Cookies!" he yipped.

"Me first."

"Aw! . . . You know me, Jimmy."

"Give me a fistful."

Gennor came into the conversation.

"Let's start our game."

"Shoot," laughed Bid.

"This is a haunted house. See? And I've come here to dig up the buried treasure."

"Do you put it in the leather bag?"

"Sure thing. The treasure is buried in this room. And I've got to dig it up and escape. You fellows are ghosts. You're to wait in the hall. And when I come from the room, you chase me. If you catch me, the treasure's yours."

"We git you."

There was a clatter of feet into the hall. The door went closed. A key clicked in the lock. Then Gennor began moving quickly about the room.

Scoop's eyes held a worried look.

"He's up to something, Jerry."

"Easy," I whispered.

"He hasn't told them about the talking frog. They would have mentioned it if they had known about it. They think it's a game. I wish I could see what he's doing."

A minute passed; two minutes.

"I can't stand it any longer," Scoop said in a strained voice. "I've got to see what he's up to."

"But if you open the door," I told him, worried, "he'll hear you and yell for his gang."

But the other was not to be stopped.

The bolt was drawn back. And quietly turning the knob, he opened the door. Then——

"Jerry! He isn't here!"

Together we ran to an open window. On the ground directly below us Gennor was coiling a long rope. He had thus made his escape, pulling the rope after him.

"The rope was in the leather bag," cried Scoop. "And he's running away with the talking frog. See? Here's the wooden box that it was buried in."

Gennor was now cutting through the weeds toward the red roadster. Throwing up the cover of the car's rear luggage box, he tossed the leather bag inside. Then he jumped into the seat.

I bounded to the door. But the key to open it wasn't in the lock.

"What's the matter in there?" Bid inquired from the hall.

"Gennor's gone out through the window," I cried.

"Who are you?"

I told him.

"If you'll help us get the talking frog from Gennor," I cried, "we'll pay you a hundred dollars."

"Go lay an egg! You haven't got a hundred cents."

"We'll have a lot of money," I cried, "if we save the talking frog. Aw, come on, fellows! We're Tutter kids. You ought to stick up for us, rather than let an outsider cheat us."

There was an excited confab in the hall.

"He brought us here to play games," said Jimmy.

"Sure thing."

"He never told us that the frog was here."

Bid hammered on the door.

"I believe you're lying. For Gennor told us yesterday that he'd give us ten dollars apiece if we'd help him find the talking frog."

"Then he's double crossing you. Yes, that's it! He brought you here to help him because he didn't dare to come in here alone. And now he's skinning out."

"The crook! Where is he?"

"He's outside," Scoop called from the window, "searching his pockets for his auto key. You can head him off if you snap into it."

A diminishing clatter of shoes came from the hall. I ran to the window. The red car was still in the yard.

"Hey!" yelled Bid, coming into sight on the run.

"I've been waiting for you," lied Gennor.

There was considerable exciting talk. We saw Gennor bring out a roll of greenbacks and pass them around. Then the whole gang got into the car. Having found his switch key, the driver started the motor. There was a clashing of gears; the car hurtled forward, quickly disappearing from our sight.

I looked at Scoop and he looked at me, but neither of us said a word. We were too sick and discouraged to talk.

We were licked now. There was no doubt of that. Almost with our hands on the talking frog, we had let Gennor slip in and get it away from us. Long before we could get to town he would be on his way to Chicago with the stolen invention.

Suddenly Scoop clutched my arm.

"Lookit!" he cried, pointing.

"Romeo!"

"And the old soap man!"

The spy and his skinny horse had come into sight at the spot where the red roadster had disappeared. Getting out of the buggy in the mill yard, the driver unhitched his horse, then came toward the hotel, carrying in one hand his soap satchel and in the other a black leather traveling bag.

Scoop made a queer throat sound.

"It's Gennor's bag!" he cried.

Clutching a chair, my now crazy companion smashed down the door into the hall.

"Jerry," he panted, his eyes shining, "our luck has changed. We still have a chance to recover the talking frog."

CHAPTER XXI

FISHING!

NOT until later, until our adventure was over with and the excitement had died out of my nerves, did I fully realize how fortunate it was for the two of us that Scoop, in good presence of mind, had smashed down the hall door in advance of the soap man's entrance into the old hotel.

For we would have been at a disadvantage, as you can see, if we had waited and the enemy had heard us smashing our way to freedom. There would have been no chance then for us to gain possible secret possession of the talking frog.

The spy had entered the hotel through the kitchen door. But we couldn't hear him in the building. And this worried us, in a measure. For we were fearful of suddenly meeting him, face to face, in the building's shadowy halls.

Of course, in meeting him we could have outrun him. Easy. We were in no particular danger. But it was necessary to our plans to not let the newcomer know that we were ahead of him in the building. This was the main reason why we didn't want to meet him.

We had descended the two flights of stairs to the ground floor and were almost to the doorway leading into the kitchen when our ears were suddenly punctured by a gurgling sneeze.

We stopped as quick as scat.

"He's in the kitchen," whispered Scoop.

"Maybe he's laying for us."

"Probably."

"What are you going to do?"

"Get a look at him if I can."

So we tiptoed to the door. But when we got there we didn't dare to put out our heads. It was too risky.

To one side of the kitchen, against the wooden wall, was a stairway leading to a room directly above. This gave us an idea. And going back up the stairs, to the second floor, we sought the room over the kitchen, hoping that we would be able to see into the room where the spy was through a knot hole in the board ceiling.

We were lucky. Not only was there many knot holes, but directly over the spy was an open trapdoor.

It took careful walking, I want to tell you. For you know how a board floor sort of groans and creaks when you step on it. We were fully three minutes crossing the room to the trapdoor. Each step was taken with extreme caution.

Below us, seated on a box, the soap man was hard at work. A dozen or more bars of soap lay on the floor at his feet. He was cutting these bars into slices. Each slice was given a few drops of perfume and then squeezed separately in an iron jigger, which seemed to be a sort of mold. In went a thin slice of soap, then squeeze, then out came a cake of Bubbles of Beauty with the name pressed into the soap just as slick as you please. The big bars on the floor were marked I-V-O-R-Y.

"What the dickens? . . ." I breathed in Scoop's ear. "Does he make his beauty soap out of *Ivory?*"

"Seems so."

I was dizzy.

"But it made Miss Prindle beautiful."

"That's what you said. I didn't see her."

"Red, too."

I couldn't understand it. It would seem on first thought that the beauty soap was a fake. Still, it couldn't be a fake, I told myself. For in the dressmaker's case, and in Red's case, too, it had done all that was claimed for it.

We had wondered what the soap man's purpose was in coming to the old hotel. We had thought, at first, that he knew something about the ghost. But now we quickly concluded that he had been selling soap in the neighborhood, and had stopped at the hotel to fix up a supply of soap for the coming day's business. There was nothing in his actions that would suggest that he knew about the ghost. His thoughts were wholly on his work.

The traveling bag that he had brought into the hotel was on the floor directly behind him. Getting a closer look at the bag, I was convinced beyond all doubt, and so was Scoop, that it was Gennor's bag. How it had come into the soap man's possession we couldn't imagine. But here it was. And we were determined to get it.

Scoop pulled a piece of fishline out of his pocket.

"If we had a hook," he grinned, "we could do some fishing."

"Anything you want," I grinned back, "just ask me for it," and I dug up a piece of wire. I don't know why I had the wire in my pocket along with my other truck. But, lucky for us, it was there.

Fastening the bent wire to the fishline, Scoop let the hook down, swinging it slowly back and forth, trying to hook the handle of the traveling bag.

"Be careful," I grinned, "and don't hook old soapy's wig."

"Keep still. How can I get a 'bite' with you talking."

"You need a bobber," I joked.

He jiggled the line up and down for several moments.

"Hot dog!" I breathed as the hooked bag was lifted from the floor.

The soap man was still at work. He didn't know that his traveling bag had "swallowed" our hook. I grinned to myself in the thought of how amazed he would be to suddenly learn that his bag had vanished.

But I grinned too soon.

With the hooked bag within a few inches of our hands, the string broke. And down went the bag, kerplunk!

The talking frog angrily awakened.

"R-r-r-a-t-s!" it rumbled, indignant over its fall. "R-r-r-a-t-s! R-r-r-a-t-s!"

Well, if ever you saw a scared man it was the spy. He pretty nearly jumped out of his skin, as the saying is. His eyes bulged like sliced marbles.

For all he knew to the contrary, the bag had suddenly come to life and had jumped into the air like a grasshopper. Maybe he believed in spooks. I don't know. Anyway, he took to his heels. A talking bag was more than he could stand.

It was funny. Oh, boy, how we laughed! Still, we didn't waste any time. Dropping through the trapdoor to the kitchen floor, we grabbed the bag and hoofed it for the river.

To this day we don't know where the soap man disappeared to or what became of his old horse and soap satchel. But it was a wise thing for him that he cleared out. Otherwise he would have landed in jail. For the officer was looking for him the following morning. If he is still alive, I imagine that he'll give Tutter a wide berth hereafter.

Coming to our boat, I whipped out my knife and cut the tie rope, wanting to get away from the pier as quickly as possible. Scoop cranked the motor. Put! put! put! Did the little old exhaust sound good to us? I'll tell the world. The spy couldn't catch us now.

Passing the Woodlawn Bay Hotel, we soon

came within sight of the bridge, a shadowy span in the early darkness. Hearing us coming, Deacon Pillpopper ran to the pier to meet us to learn how we had come out and to help us put the boat away.

It was after nine o'clock when we came into town. And when we rounded the hotel corner, there sat Gennor in his red automobile, directly under a street light, sort of posing important-like for the benefit of the common, everyday people passing along the sidewalk.

But his pushed-up chest went punctured when we hurried by, carrying the leather bag. Oh, boy, did his eyes bulge! But he kept shut. For he had sense enough to realize that he was licked.

Scoop chuckled.

"I wish I could have seen his face when he discovered the empty luggage box. I'll bet he felt sick."

We learned afterwards that the red car struck a bad bump shortly after it had disappeared from our sight. No doubt the bag was thrown from the car into the road, where it was picked up by the soap man.

I suspect it is a wonder to Gennor to this day how the bag came into our hands.

He left town that night, headed for Chicago.

That is the last we ever saw of him. And moreover that is the last we ever want to see of him or any boy like him.

For, as Scoop says, the fun of being rich lies in doing good turns for other and less fortunate people. And when a fellow gets Gennor's idea that money is something to lift himself above other people, he's all wrong. Without his money he might have been a good kid. For he was smart. But with his money he was a fizzle. And that is why I hope that he'll forever keep out of my way.

When we came even with the town hall, Scoop paused, letting his face go thoughtful.

"I think that we better make a prisoner of the talking frog, Jerry. For, with all of the trouble that we've had recovering it, we certainly don't want to fumble and again lose it. I can't feel that it's wholly safe in our hands. And the better plan will be to put it where a thief won't be able to get it."

"Is it your idea," I laughed, "to ask Bill Hadley to lock it up in one of his steel jail cages?"

"Why not?" grinned Scoop, starting for the door.

Seated at his desk, the town marshal gave us a questioning look when we entered.

Scoop's request brought a hearty laugh.

"How'd it be," grinned Bill, good-natured-like, "if I locked your valuable bag in the big office safe?"

"That suits me," nodded Scoop.

A twinkle came into Bill's eyes as he took the bag and hefted it.

"What have you got in it?" he questioned. "A gold brick?"

"A talking frog," informed Scoop; and he gave a quick account of our adventures.

"Well, I swan!" exploded Bill, staring at us with admiring eyes. "If you hain't the beatin'est kids I ever heard tell of. One time it's a whispering mummy that you're chasin', and the next time it's a rose-colored cat. Now it's a talkin' frog."

Then the conversation turned to the ghost.

"Of course," waggled Scoop, "I may be all wrong about the ghost's identity."

"I hope you hain't," Bill said, grim-like. "Fur I'd like to see this murder mystery cleared up. Anyway, we'll soon find out who the ghost is," and locking the frog in the office safe, he started heavily for the door, motioning for us to follow him.

CHAPTER XXII

WE CAPTURE THE GHOST

THAT night we captured the ghost, only Bill did the most of the capturing. Being the town marshal, we let him take the lead.

Shortly after our signal had brought Tom and Peg from the brick house, the ghost came creeping up the path from the road, wrapped in a sheet. Finding the kitchen door unlocked, he disappeared into the silent house. Then a light shone through the cellar windows. When the ghost came up the cellar stairs, Bill nabbed him.

It was, as Scoop had suspected, old Mr. Matson. He was carrying in his arms a wooden box, similar in size to the box that we had used in burying the talking frog. And when the box was opened, what do you know if it wasn't crammed full of greenbacks and silver dollars and five-dollar and ten-dollar gold pieces! Thousands of dollars! A bigger pile of money I never expect to see.

The captured man did a lot of screeching and

clawing. He called us robbers. And we failed to make him understand that we were not, because he was pretty much out of his head.

But he wasn't so loony but what he had remembered the hidden money. And it was to dig up the treasure that he had persistently tried to enter the brick house. The one time that he did get in, he carried off the talking frog by mistake, having dug in the wrong spot.

It was learned afterwards that in his wanderings he had been in New York City. Struck by an automobile, an operation had been performed on his head. The doctors declared that upon his entrance into the hospital he was as crazy as a loon. And I rather imagine that he was. For only a truly crazy man would spill hog blood all over his house to make the neighbors think that he had been murdered. But the operation drove much of the craziness out of the injured one's head. And remembering the buried money, he had returned to get it. Not wanting to be seen and recognized by people who thought him dead, he sought to hide from sight in the old Windmere House.

His capture gave the Tutter people something to talk about. He went to live with Mrs. Kelly, and she has charge of his money. Some day, of course, everything that he owns will be Frances Matson's.

The ten-ring puzzle was sent to Milwaukee, to the company interested in Mr. Ricks' talking frog, and they wrote back saying that they would be very glad to manufacture the puzzle in quantities and market it. I understand that Mrs. Kelly is to get a royalty check twice a year.

Mr. Ricks bought the brick house with a part of the money paid to him by the Milwaukee company, who are now building a small factory in Tutter to manufacture talking toys and puzzles. Tom, who will always be one of my warmest friends, says that he is going to be the manager of the factory when he grows up.

So you can see what *he* intends to do when *he* gets rich.

On the day that his pa and Aunt Polly returned to Tutter with their patent papers a letter was received from the president of the Gennor Radio Corporation.

Mr. Gennor said that he deeply regretted that his son, in offering to buy the talking frog and promising a factory to the townspeople, had acted without authority. And he denied employing spies to steal the invention.

In this he undoubtedly told the truth. For what we thought was a spy was just a silly old soap peddler, who had gotten the idea somehow that his dead brother had hidden a lot of money in the stone wall of his mill. No doubt Mr. Ricks misplaced the roll of dress patterns on the train. He's pretty good at misplacing things! Aunt Polly says that he would misplace his head if it wasn't fastened to him.

Dad says that big companies do business on the square. And Dad knows.

We called on Mrs. Crandon the following day. And when we had told her about our adventure she showed us her pile of soap. Twenty-four cakes!

"Did he try to make you pay for it?"

"No. The first thing I knew he was gone."

Scoop grinned.

"This ought to be enough soap to keep you beautiful for the next fifty years."

"Yes," returned Mrs. Crandon, "I heard how it beautified Miss Prindle," and she looked at me and smiled.

Dog-gone! I felt pretty cheap. For everybody in town knew the joke. The woman I had seen on Miss Prindle's porch was her out-of-town sister. And Red's beauty was all put on with cold cream and face powder. He had his mother fix him up to fool me.

The Strickers, of course, had made up the fake beauty letter.

"Anyway," laughed Mrs. Crandon, "the soap is good soap, whether it makes people beautiful or not. It has such a good smell that the baby bit into a cake yesterday afternoon, thinking it was candy, I suppose, and I was up half the night with her."

"If the baby has warts on the inside of her stomach," grinned Scoop, "she's cured for life. For Bubbles of Beauty is death on warts. If you think I'm stringing you, ask Jerry. The soap cured the wart that Mrs. Pederson put on the top of his head with a broom."

"If you don't dry up," I waggled, "I'll put a wart on your head."

But he knew I said it in fun, for I was grinning.

THE END

THE JERRY TODD SERIES

By LEO EDWARDS

Illustrated. Individual Colored Wrappers For Each Story
Every Volume Complete in Itself

Detective stories for boys! Jerry Todd and his trusty pals solve many a baffling mystery in their home town, much to the amusement of all who read of their adventures.

JERRY TODD AND THE WHISPERING MUMMY

Having been duly appointed "Juvenile Jupiter Detectives" Jerry Todd and his trusty pals little realize how fast things are going to happen. First comes the amazing adventure in the museum in Tutter College. Did the mummy actually whisper? And did it later vanish of its own accord?

JERRY TODD AND THE ROSE-COLORED CAT

Cats by the dozens; cats by the hundreds; and most important of all, a mysterious five-hundred dollar rose-colored cat. Then comes the lamentable accident to Lady Victoria's aristocratic tail; the operation; the overdose of chloroform; the funeral. There is a laugh on every page.

JERRY TODD AND THE OAK ISLAND TREASURE

Jerry Todd and his pals set themselves up in the show business by transforming a disused clay scow of Mr. Todd's into a floating theatre. And a very wonderful show it is! Certainly it leads the boys into exceptional adventures.

JERRY TODD AND THE WALTZING HEN

That strange hen? Why does it waltz? And what is the secret of the prowling peril? Then, even as the Hindu had earlier died so quickly and mysteriously, the boys' old friend disappears. Then comes the final ludicrous climax.

JERRY TODD AND THE TALKING FROG

Jerry Todd and his chums leagued together to help another boy save a peculiar invention of his father's, a talking frog, from thieving hands,—wait breathlessly in the lonely brick house where the puzzle maker had met with such a strange death. Fun and mystery here!

GROSSET & DUNLAP, PUBLISHERS, NEW YORK